FRIENDS OF APIS RADIO

Fabulist Fiction Tales

Joan d'Arc

Huntergatheress Publishing, Providence, Rhode Island

ISBN-13: 9798642530597
ISBN-10: 1477123456

Cover design by: Art Painter
Library of Congress Control Number: 2018675309
Printed in the United States of America

Black bee cover graphic by Harry Strauss, Pixabay.com

Hear now of particles existing in the world
And yet cannot be warped nor twirled
The particles of speech your sound surrounds
And space between the particles abounds
We never see it coming toward the nose
The particles of that which make a rose
Hear me now proclaim!
Things cannot be made from nothing nor unmade
But used and cast back into god's design
Where unseen it meets a glitch in the stitch of time

JOAN D'ARC, CHRONOSQUIRE

To Paul,
In friendship,
Joan d'Arc

CONTENTS

INTRODUCTION

Friends of Apis Radio by Joan d'Arc is a work of fabulism and supernatural horror. Fabulism is a form of magical realism in which fantastical elements are imposed onto an everyday setting. This sub-genre combines science fiction, horror, realism and fairytale. It looks at the mundane through a magical, supernatural lens as it moves through multiple planes of reality. It brings fables, folk tales and myths into contemporary social relevance.

Fed from a deep-rooted dread of death and an uncomfortable sense of humor regarding taboo themes, Joan d'Arc's fabulist tales lure the reader into an aberrant world, ferried by a surrogate psychopomp in an unconventional transport, such as a pneumatic tube, a carpet of bees, or an antique locomotive. Once in the sway of the untrustworthy other, the characters are beguiled, misled on a fantastical trip.

In a writing style rich in aerial movement and numinous trickster guides, this fabulist short story collection from *Paranoia Magazine's* Joan d'Arc squeezes you between the elevator doors and yells, "Going up!"

Here are fourteen tales featuring monstrous honey bees, an undead swindler, squid computer geeks and hungry teenage aliens—surrealism and supernatural horror never used this much super glue.

Joan d'Arc's speculative fiction follows decades of writings on supernatural, occult, UFO, and Forteana subjects, dozens of which were published in such collections as *Paranoia, UFO Magazine, Namaste, Secret and Suppressed II, The Universal Seduction, Wake Up Down There!, UFO Digest*, and in her own books listed in the back of this book.

ABOUT THE AUTHOR

Joan d'Arc's fiction has appeared in *Danse Macabre, The Wedding Cake House Anthology* and *Huntergatheress Journal*. Her non-fiction work has been published in *Paranoia Magazine, UFO Magazine, Namaste Magazine* (UK), *Secret and Suppressed II, The Universal Seduction, UFO Digest, Wake Up Down There!, LaGazette Forteenne* (in French) and *Hellraiser Homemaker, the Gonzo Domestic Survival Guide.*

She is the past publisher of *Paranoia Magazine* (1992–2012), *Newspeak Katazine* (1995-1997) and *Hunter-Gatheress Journal* (Vol. 1, 2008, Vol. 2, 2009), published in Providence, Rhode Island. She is the author of *Space Travelers and the Genesis of the Human Form,* and *Phenomenal World,* both published by The Book Tree, and *Conspiracy Geek,* published by Sisyphus Press. She is the co-editor of *The Conspiracy Reader* and *The New Conspiracy Reader,* translated into Japanese and Romanian.

FRIENDS OF APIS RADIO

It all seemed so long ago to Wintu now, the years of fallow crops from the white lines that crisscrossed the sky. He remembered the day Father shaded his eyes from the baking sun and said, "the white man is on another killing spree. He has killed all the bees, and now he's killing off the rest of us."

Wintu grew shrewd and fast on his feet; he outran and outsmarted the Haters. At first, the Haters stayed outside the reservation. By the time Wintu was ten years old, they had moved inside the reservation, taking things that weren't theirs to take.

One night, a Hater smashed the window and climbed into their kitchen. Father rose up quickly. The Hater swung at him with a bat, hitting him in the stomach. Father grabbed a heavy wooden chair and struck him powerfully on the head, knocking him unconscious.

Hearing the commotion, Wintu ran in and helped drag the body outside. "This is how you get the rest of them to leave you alone," Father said, as he dropped the body in the street. He bent down and lit the man's shirt with a match. His clothing went up in flames; his charred body smelled like cooked meat.

"He will be done when he's done. Let the Haters eat his body. We never eat the body of a Hater, no matter how hungry we are."

Father was never the same after he was struck in the stomach. Mama called Doctor Hain to his bedside. "Leroy has internal bleeding, Emma," he said. "Is it okay for me to talk in front of Wenona and Wintu?"

Emma answered, "They have seen so much, and they have had to grow up fast." She put an arm around each of them. "We would like the truth about Leroy, so we know how to plan for his absence."

Wintu felt a gut punch as if the Hater had hit him the same. He bowed his head and listened to Doctor Hain.

"There are no hospitals running. Everything has broken down. You can keep him comfortable here." Doctor Hain stayed the day, showing them how to change the dressing on the wound, which was deep and infected.

That night Doctor Hain organized a meeting with the tribal council and all members of the Kickapoo reservation. He stood at the podium and explained what was going on with the hate disease. "There is a sanctuary called Friends of Apis. They have studied this disease. They believe the poison chemtrails that killed the bees are killing humans slowly through a brain disease they have named ProtoH8. They say the word 'Proto' stands for 'the first' disease of its kind, and H-eight is short for hate."

Marlin Brady held her youngest child crying on her lap. She shouted from the back. "Will we catch this disease too?"

"You likely have it already," said Doctor Hain. He felt a shock ripple through the crowd. "A scant population might walk between the raindrops, I'm told. But I have some good news. The doctors at

Friends of Apis have developed a cure made from the bee's powerful venom. They have told me we should go there and accept the bee's gift."

"Is this H-eight disease killing all the animals we've seen?" asked Hadwin Nash. He had hunted since he was knee high, and he had never seen a disease waste large animals over the earth like this killer had done.

"The animals are dying of starvation, not ProtoH8," said the doctor. "The animals can't find anything to eat, same as you. This group, the Friends of Apis, has taken many species of wildlife into their sanctuary. They have many bee species, including *Apis mellifera*, the honeybee. They are growing food to feed thousands of people. They welcome all of you to their center for the cure."

"How would I know if I have the disease?" asked Marin Scott, raising her bone thin arm in the air and waving her open palm.

"You don't know for sure," said Doctor Hain. "You can carry the disease for many years, and it won't have this effect on you—the killer instinct you've seen. But I am told 99 percent of you are carrying it. You just have to believe me when I tell you. I invite you to follow me to the sanctuary tomorrow and accept the bee's gift."

People began to talk with those next to them. Doctor Hain cleared his throat loudly. "But you may not like what I have to say next!" They stopped chatting. He made sure everyone was looking at him before he continued. "Once you are cleared of the disease, you must remain at Friends of Apis, so you don't become re-infected. You can't come back here." He motioned down to this ground, this home, this community that was all they had ever known.

Shouting broke out amongst the tribe. He

waved his arms and hollered over the racket, "If you stay here, you will slowly starve to death. Those are your options."

Leroy Windsong passed away four days later, and a funeral was held in the chapel. The tribal elders decided everyone should live under the same roof, so they could fight off the Haters together.

"We won't go to the bee sanctuary just yet," Emma said to Wenona and Wintu, as they packed up their things.

◆ ◆ ◆

"Wenona, please water the sunflowers!" Grampa shouted, as she slammed the screen door to the farmhouse and bounded down the stairs.

"Sure, Grampa Slim. I'm doing that." *Except I don't know this Grampa. I don't know any Grampa.*

She steered clear of that weird Bear Boone, as he watered his sickly beehive under the red maple. His shadow towered across the burnt yard, folded in the middle and angled up the side of the barn. Bear's face was covered by the white net of the Beekeeper, but Wenona could feel his eyes follow her as she walked toward the well.

Old bumble body, always futzing with that thing. She stooped at the spigot to fill the watering pail, eyeing him through straight, black hair falling across her angular, brown face. The Beekeeper raised his arm to the hard-boiled sun. She shaded her eyes in the direction of the wonderment she saw then, when the sky ripped open and black things fell out.

"Don't be concerned," she heard in her head. A honeybee began looping around her, changing directions, and looping the other way. More bees circled her hands and she dropped her water pail. As a dark swarm flowed in from her periphery, she looked for the shortest route to safety. *Run, legs, run*, she thought, but her legs weren't running.

The swarm picked her up by the neck like a kitten—she dangled in still life, not knowing. Not knowing what to do with her legs. Not knowing how to sit in the sky. The thick carpet moved beneath her, molding to her form.

The crumbling roof of the farmhouse rushed by below, and the sunflowers in their struggling patch raised their crowned faces to watch her float past. She saw Bear pick up his rifle and climb into his green pickup truck. As she rose higher, she saw him racing north, his tires kicking up a column of dust. But she couldn't even care about that, or about her chores, or about anything, as she sped over the flat landscape of dead wheat fields; over silos spilling with rotting corn; over dried-up ponds and bloated bodies of dead cows.

And she couldn't even care.

Bear Boone knew every meandering, country road to the Kickapoo reservation on the Kansas border with Nebraska. He sped around a curve between long-dead cornfields. *Just one more pass*, he thought. He listened to Dr. Jack Barnes on Friends of Apis Radio.

They are still trickling in after a year of intensive undertaking, but we've got to step up the pace. We're on the line of life and death. Please get all children to a safe house.

He pulled up in front of the tribal council office and took his pistol out of the glove box. He had gotten the last group out of here about a week ago, but he had a nagging feeling. Was there a boy named Wintu?

Bear crept around the back of the building. A Hater holding a tire iron limped around the corner; ragged clothes hanging on his spare frame, face mottled with crusty blood. On the inside he was rabid, agitated, paranoid. He had an unscratchable itch for mayhem. He was in the full throes of the disease.

Bear flattened himself against the brown log building. The white beekeeping suit with the black and gold Friends of Apis emblem on the chest rarely made good camouflage. Once the Hater caught sight of him, the rage came on like a spastic orgasm. He convulsed toward him with the tire iron raised, his skinny arms barely able to swing. Bear settled him mid-charge; then, three, clean pistol shots to the limbic plumbing for good measure. He considered it a service.

On the opposite side of the street, a barefoot boy stepped out of the laundry center. His black hair almost touched his shoulders; his grubby clothes hugged his slight body. Looking across, he spied the green truck—the one he saw when his family had disappeared. He heard three shots as he climbed into the open back.

Wintu had been here alone since his family left. At dusk, he quietly wandered the edges of the group looking for food. Lone Haters would continuously band, brawl, disband; fighting over food, but mostly over nothing. If he avoided looking them in the eye, he could sneak a hotdog or a sandwich, so his belly wouldn't hurt, and he could sleep at night.

But that wouldn't stop the nightmares of the broken madmen in his midst, who crushed each other's skulls for no worse than he had done.

Bear crossed the street and went into the laundry center with his pistol drawn. In the back office, a man's head was split halfway open with a hatchet stuck in it. The bathroom was empty. He came out and crossed over toward the café, spying a movement in the back of the truck. He picked up Wintu with one arm and put him in front with him.

The next morning, Grampa Slim made breakfast for Wintu and found him some shoes. Wintu watched Bear water the sick beehive with sugar water. Bear pointed at the sky and a black cloud zigzagged down, taking Wintu with no concern over the parched earth.

Wenona opened one eye and read the sign on the door: "Dr. Jack Barnes."

She drew a blank on how she had arrived on this bench. She wondered if someone had found her and dropped her off here—a stranger paying a kindness, or maybe it was Bear Boone. She half expected to see him come around the corner, but when he didn't show, she rose and turned the doorknob.

She took the only empty seat in the waiting room; everyone seemed to be asleep. The nurse behind the glass rapped loudly on the window, pointing to the sign-in register. She signed "Wenona Windsong," and sat down.

The walls were of a golden, hexagonal texture that glistened brightly. The light came from the ceiling, and the ceiling was the sky. It was hard to focus on any one thing because the room was turning and swaying in a sweet smelling breeze. The radio was between stations, droning static.

Wenona eyed the brown lady next to her in the blue sweater, her long, bronze hair wrapped up on top of her head. "Do we all have a sickness?" she asked. She glanced down at her own legs; her shorts were torn, sandals broken, knees scraped. A few minutes later, she persisted. "Who made this appointment for me, anyway? I mean, it's sure quizzical, right?"

Wenona heard Bear's voice, and she had no fight against the ensuing power nap. Following that nap, she got a refreshed feeling and started to eyeball the other patients and—come to see it now, as she hadn't seen it earlier—she recognized some of them. Paladin had been at the farm a few days; about the same for Clem. Dyani had helped with the chores, and so had Salem, but then they were gone. Now here they were. The closer she looked at them the more tired she became. Sleep grabbed at her wits, and Bear's voice cut in over the radio static, saying it was not her concern.

Shocked awake by a bang on the glass, Wenona walked across the room. Opening the door, she nearly collided with an enormous black and gold honeybee in a white nurse's dress who emitted a buzzing sound that resembled her name. She felt oddly calm about meeting a bipedal insect that was about her own height. The nurse gazed at Wenona with black, searching eyes that took up the entire front of her face.

She offered her hand—slender and furry, with four fingers and a thumb—and said her name was Muriel. Walking in low-strung strides across the room, she motioned with fluttering arms to an exam table.

Muriel gave Wenona a sweet, warm drink. "Don't be afraid. You are with friends here. We are the Friends of Apis." she said, with a voice that hummed from a deep place. Her immense, fuzzy head swiveled and cocked to one side. "How old are you, youngster?"

"I just turned 16," she replied, not knowing whether to look up into the immense, beguiling eyes, or straight into the barrel-shaped chest, vibrating with sound, or to the mouth, small and unmoving. Or was there a mouth? In the nurse's black, reflective eyes, Wenona caught her own stunned reflection.

Muriel helped her undress and tied the johnnie in the back. She described the catastrophic collapse of the bee colonies, the sickness and vile transgressions of humankind, the slow starvation of the animals. She said the chemicals in the skies had caused the human brain disease, ProtoH8. "In late stages of the disease," she said, "if you survive that long, the disease moves to the brain's limbic system, resulting in severe personality changes and violent behavior."

Muriel explained the renewal that would come if she accepted the bee's gift. Wenona had heard this talk before. Deep memories began to stir. Muriel turned a dark, hypnotic eye toward her. Transfixed, Wenona felt herself falling into a pitch-black pit, her heart beating violently against her chest.

As Muriel pulled her close to her fuzzy face, her voice box bumbled, "I believe you can do wondrous things in the new world that's coming, if you accept the bee's gift. I want you to be safe here with us. You can do this. Okay?"

They nodded in unison.

"Please lay on your stomach and breathe through the face cutout," Muriel said. "Doctor Jack will be in shortly."

Wenona struggled to throw off the heaviness that inebriated her senses. She had tried to remember where she lived before the farm, but every time she tried to recall that part of her life, Bear Boone had thrown on another wet blanket of control. As she rested, a locked memory edged its way clearly to the front. In it, she joggled back and forth to the rumble of a motor. She opened one eye. She was slouched in the bed of a green pick-up with some other native children. She rolled her eye toward her left shoulder; the woman leaning on it was her mother. Their trouble with the Haters was over, but where was her mother now?

Another memory opened up. Doctor Hain had come to the reservation to take care of her father's stomach wound. He said the Friends of Apis had developed a cure from the bee venom, and they should all go there and accept the bee's gift. Nobody went with him. They lost many to the disease. To starvation. And to pride.

Doctor Jack entered the room and slammed the door shut. He straightaway began pricking the bottom of her feet with sharp needles. After each prick, there was a quivering, flapping sensation. It moved to the legs, then up her spine. She shouted out and the pain subsided.

When he was done treating the rear side, Doctor Jack assisted her in turning over, and she saw that he was an elderly, but quite immense, worker bee. He was at least a foot taller than Muriel, much broader and enormously bulky. Shock white tufts of hair shot out around captivating lenses that took up the front of his head. Wenona was unable to look away from her own horrified reflection in the mirrors of his lidless eyes. It was as if she were nailed to the table, as tiny bees pinched and stung her legs, moving up to her stomach and arms.

Swiftly, the doctor packed the bees into a mini hive inside his brown doctor bag. He took a big brush and coated her with a sticky syrup. She was startled by the deep hum that commingled with his speech, like a broken radio speaker, while his two antennae gestured in the air to phantom signals. "Wenona, this is royal jelly," he explained, as he wrapped her tightly in a white blanket. "It will help you with the itching and swelling caused by the disease toxins your cells have dumped out. Sleep now."

But the doctor didn't go. As she slipped under, the surgery team entered.

◆ ◆ ◆

Wenona awoke in a fugue state. No information. No memory. No sound. Just four walls and a ceiling of white. *I have died*, she thought.

The next realization was pain—if death were painless, this could not be it. A drumbeat pounded at her temples. Every small exertion inflicted a deep, searing muscle pain. "Hello! Is anyone there?" she cried out, her voice echoing in damp air. Beads of thick liquid dribbled down the walls. She put a finger up to it. The taste was both sweet and spicy. She ate more.

There was filtered light at the top; *maybe a window*, she thought. Pushing past the hurt, she took a deep breath and reached up. A thin skin enclosed the opening; she tried to push on it, but it was sealed tight as a drum. She settled back, immobilized, weak. As she rested, she became aware that the overbearing static of the waiting room had been replaced by a chatter of distinct voices.

You are listening to Friends of Apis Radio.

A child's voice asked, *How can I become a field operator?*

Another child asked, *Why did your father choose the bee as our soul mate?*

Wenona wondered, *How am I hearing the radio now?*

The answer came in Muriel's voice with astonishing clarity. The voice was all around her and inside her head. *Because you are part of the Mind now. All you have to do is think, and the rest of us can hear you. Isn't that grand?*

Wenona looked around the small cell. Muriel wasn't there. *I should warn you,* Wenona thought. *You might not like some of my thoughts.*

Muriel laughed. *The best thing is you will learn to be a nicer person.*

Doctor Jack's voice came in now; a robust buzzing sound that shook the walls and made her head vibrate.

Field operators can use the Hive Mind to exert control during capture and transfer. Some have said our tactics are coercive and heavy handed. We have our reasons—one is for our own protection. The survivors have the disease but aren't yet exhibiting violent behavior. That could change at any time.

Wenona realized he was talking about Bear Boone. She thought, *He's not the enemy. If I ever see him again, I'll have to apologize for being so wicked.*

Muriel responded. *See, Wenona. You are already becoming nicer. And I think he heard you. Our thoughts in the Mind are instantaneous.*

◆ ◆ ◆

The next day, Wenona's younger brother would meet Muriel. He was so nervous he stuttered. "My n-n-name is Wintu Windsong."

"And how old are you, Wintu?" asked Muriel.

"T-t-twelve," he answered. "Ma'am, are you a human or a bee?"

Muriel answered, "I'm part *Homo sapiens* and part *Apis mellifera*, the honeybee. I'm called an Apsape."

"I'd like to become a Beekeeper, like Bear Boone, Ma'am."

"Right now, our field operators are Apsapes, like me," Muriel said. "As special creations, we are immune to the ProtoH8 disease. Normally, once cured, all boys must remain inside the beehive sanctuary, and they must choose a work program—either tending the animals or planting the gardens. But I might have another program I can put you in."

Muriel went to Jack. "He has the antibodies. Shall we send him to Parthenon?"

"Yes, of course. Prepare him."

Doctor Jack relaxed in his hive pod and listened to transcripts from his father's genetics research. He liked to borrow a quote for his radio chats—the historical forays made the Hive Mind light up. Here was a new one he hadn't heard before; his antenna perked up and he bumbled out loud.

It was a meeting at the Friends of Apis laboratory between Dr. Bingham Barnes, Dr. Josey Chan, and field operator, Arthur Cloot. Josey was a human like Jack's father, Bingham. Jack remembered her well; she had a jarring and unpleasant personality, but she was his father's closest work partner, never far from his side.

"Mr. Cloot," said Josey. "We brought you in to discuss our new goals relative to your work with *Homo sapiens*. We are transferring the *Apis sapiens* genetics program out of the laboratory and into our spacious new maternity hives."

"And how can I help you with that?" Arthur asked.

"Bring us more human females," replied Josey.

"Why can't you mate the Apsape drones and queens for that program?"

"You should already know this, Arthur!" Josey replied with obvious annoyance. "Apsapes are genetic hybrids. They cannot produce offspring. We need more human implant vessels."

Bingham Barnes interrupted. "Please, Arthur. Can we just talk about our urgent needs for the new real estate?"

Doctor Jack deleted the transcript from the Mind.

"Do you want to store it in the banks?" asked the Mind.

"No," he answered.

He lowered his huge head and closed his lenses, brought a furry hand up to stroke his forehead. He recalled Father's utopian quackery, his God mania. The disagreement played out in his mind again.

"Father, the potential consequences of this plan are indefensible," he had shouted in a rage. "How can you let the cure to a disease devastate the entire future of *Homo sapiens*?"

Father retorted, angrily, "How can I let a disease end the highly successful and innovative genius of the human mind? It can carry on in another body type. But I see you have a racial prejudice."

"I do not," young Jack answered, walking out of the lab in a huff. But it wasn't true, and his father knew it. As a child, Jack had despised the Hive Mind. Inborn and ever present, it was an interloper, a bad twin. He felt molested by its tenacious grip. He tried to determine its location so he could chop it off like a scurvy hand, pull it out like a crooked spine. It always knew about his anti-communal urges and tried to challenge them. He would hum loudly to drown it out.

There had been a few human children in the first Friends of Apis genetic trial, allowed to run freely amongst the pedigreed Apsapes. These had been Jack's schoolmates. As the children grew, a cultural war reared its head. The dominant Apsape culture treated the Homosape children like aliens from another planet. The Apsape children teased them for being alone in their big empty heads, for having to learn everything the slow way, by rote. They taunted them in a song about teeny-weeny eyes that couldn't see on the wind, little funnel ears that couldn't hear in the Mind.

Conceited and smug, the little Homosapes always had a different opinion than the others. Worse, once the young Apsapes learned there was such a thing as a self, the idea underpinned a revolution the elders had to nip in the bud. Some Apsape youngsters secretly searched for a vestigial organ of identity and found only an inert prune. They wondered how it worked. They tried it out clumsily and were outed in the Mind, scorned in the halls of group think, and deleted, post haste.

The cultural war angered Bingham Barnes. "This experiment is done! It's far too dangerous," he had ranted. "The Hive Mind takes the place of government, school, work, sex, entertainment. All of it! The Apsape culture has no room for autonomy. It has no place for humans!"

With Father gone now, Jack had begun a covert experiment; a new colony that didn't separate human males and females. But Parthenon did separate humans from Apsapes.

There were no Apsapes allowed.

Wenona's mind was at peace. Rays of gold and orange seeped through her lids, large shadows played on the wall. Now she grasped the meaning of the outside bumble-babble. *Give her a drink. Feed her.* Long, hairy arms washed her face with water, gave her nectar inside a white tulip and mashed food inside a corn husk. The first bite opened lost memories of beans and squash, the next was apples and peaches. The pain receded, and her strength returned.

More commands issued from above. *Get her dressed for battle.* They dressed her in body armor. With hardly a beat, the strange arms yanked her straight up and out of her cell, and she was rocked by the vision before her: a colossal Apsape queen towered over an army of five-foot drones, flapping their wings in a shrill commotion. The queen's lieutenant placed a sword and shield into Wenona's hands and pushed her through the crowd.

The drones surrounded the two of them in a circle. The queen dwarfed Wenona by at least two feet. She stared at the queen's thorax, not knowing where to look or what to do. *Come to me, my child*, the queen beckoned. Her gaze was like opium. She was old and fat, but her mental prowess was devastating.

Wenona looked up into the queen's eye and flashed back to Muriel. There was a new world coming, she had said. "I want you to be safe here with us." As she stared, dumbfounded, the queen went from zero to sixty, piercing her arm with a short, sharp jab of her handheld stinger.

Wenona pulled out of her daze, shrieking, "Oh no, lady. I'm not coming to you!"

She whirled around, defending the stabs with her shield. She used the sword against the queen's stinger, pushing it down, knocking it up and away. They moved in a circle—lunged, chopped, defended, stepped back.

At each twirl, the queen's head swiveled to lock on to the fierce, little human. They circled in the opposite direction. The movements exhausted the aging queen. She became dizzy and lashed out wildly, missing her target.

The huge drones whooped, shrieked—crowded in. Closer. Closer. Wenona heard their flightless wings rubbing together, smelled their musky libido.

Come to me, my darling!, the queen wept softly. She tried to take a step forward, but nothing worked anymore. An awful shriek arose, paining every head in the Mind. *You are my baybeeeee!*

Wenona tacked quickly in the opposite direction. The queen stumbled and fell on her back, her arms and legs flapping helplessly.

Please don't do it, little one, she whimpered.

Wenona took a few pokes with her sword trying to locate the soft abdomen. Then, holding the onyx blade high in the air, she drove it forcefully into the queen's belly. Her glistening entrails spurted up into the air and plopped down onto her mountainous body, causing whoops of pleasure amongst the rabble.

The drones slurped the delicacy, as her death burble spread through the Mind. They pulled out her twitching arms and legs and sucked on them ravenously. They chomped through her middle cavity, while her thorax hummed her last song. They fought over her shining innards, as her all-seeing eyes went dead.

Wintu ran into the warm night, staying on the lit paths of the beehive sanctuary as Muriel had told him. When he arrived at the metal fencing, he looked for the section that would give way. There it was, just as she had described. He slipped under the loose section of wire and was free. He stopped running when his side ached. "You will go down 2000 golden stairs," Muriel said.

His breath caught in his throat when he saw the stairs, gleaming brightly against the night sky. They dipped down forever and disappeared into the clouds. He tried the first few stairs and they bounced a little. Were they made of wax? He tried to take them quickly but only tumbled down, striking his head painfully. His legs grew weary as he lost count of the stairs. A heavy mist of clouds obscured his view. He tripped again and tumbled down, rested a moment. He ate a honey sandwich and arose. His legs wobbled on each step. His thigh muscles began to ache. Where was the end of this thing?

As the sun began to rise over the horizon, Wintu finally fell exhausted at the bottom of the golden stairway. He rested and caught his gasping breath. He turned to look and the stairway was gone. Had he imagined it? He pushed on, entering a heavily wooded area with low trees and prickly bushes. Pushing through the brush with his hands, he came to a clearing. Just ahead was the main road Muriel had told him to follow, saying, "Beware of the Beekeepers, who will be out looking for you."

The sun shone with an exacting vengeance now, shriveling every leaf in its sight. He trudged in the sand of the roadside, his toes throbbing mercilessly in the tight shoes. There was no spittle now to quench the killer thirst that parched his throat. He had eaten all his honey sandwiches, and he didn't know what was supposed to happen. He was to look for a place called Parthenon. Up ahead, there was a car pulled over, and as he approached, he saw a young woman in the passenger seat.

"Excuse me," Wintu said. "Would you possibly have a drink of water?"

Startled, she began screaming. A young man asleep in the back sat up and grabbed his gun. "Get away from us," he shouted.

"Don't shoot. I don't mean any trouble," Wintu replied, holding his arms in the air. "I just left a place called Friends of Apis."

"Put down the gun, Danny," she said. "He's just a kid."

"Are you a Protohead?" asked Danny.

"I'm not a Protohead. I'm cured."

The man got out of the backseat slowly. His blonde hair was long and shaggy, his large pants held up with a tight belt. He tossed Wintu a bottle of water. "You come from Friends of Apis?"

"Yeah. They have a treatment there for the Proto Hate disease."

"What are you doing here, then? Did you escape?" Danny asked.

"No. They said I was special, and I should go to Parthenon."

"I never heard of anyone leaving Friends of Apis in one piece, let lone a boy wandering around alive!" said Danny.

"Shut up, Danny!" said the woman. "Well, what's your name, kid? We're looking for Parthenon too."

"I'm Wintu."

"Get in the back, Wintu. I'm Pearl."

Wintu was exhausted and slept nearly two hours. He sat up and peered out the back window. On the horizon above the clouds, the sun glinted off the monstrous, golden beehive structures—a luring beacon with a hideous secret.

"What's it like there?" asked Pearl.

"It's not as beautiful as it looks from here. It's like a work prison. The boys have to tend the animals and gardens. I don't know what the girls do."

"Who told you that?"

"Muriel told me. She's an Apsape; a human bee. Honestly, a walking bee!"

Pearl looked at Danny and shivered. "About those Beekeepers in the white suits," said Pearl. "Do you know whose side they're on?"

"I dunno. I only met one. A medicine man named Bear Boone. He pulls the bees from the sky and carries you to Friends of Apis."

At dusk, they pulled over to stretch their limbs under the night sky. There had been a few turns on the road, and Wintu pointed the way. He didn't know how he knew. Pearl gave him a bulky sweater and a blanket, and she began to make a bed on a soft patch of moss for her and Danny. That's when Wintu noticed she had a baby in her belly.

"Thank you, Pearl," said Wintu. "I have to take a pee."

"Don't go far," Pearl warned.

The woods were quiet as he walked on the path toward the large pines. He sneaked in behind the first group of trees. As he peed on a mound of pine needles, Wintu heard leaves crunching around him. Sticks breaking. Something big walking around. The noise surrounded him. He wondered what type of large animal could still be alive in these woods.

As he returned to the path, he was startled by an immense, white shape standing in front of him. "Muriel sent me to Parthenon, and you can't stop me!" he shouted at Bear Boone.

A quaking buzz broke free of Bear's chest. *"I'm not here to stop you. I've been guiding your way!"*

Startled by the blaring treble that saturated his skull, Wintu began running back to his friends. "How are you inside my head? Get away from me!" he cried.

Bear stopped him in his tracks. His words buzzed and sawed chaotically through Wintu's head like a chainsaw symphony.

Freedom is a precarious thing! A human with

the hate disease, even treated, can become vio-
lent again, reinfected from the open air. We wish
we could do better outside of the Beehive, but
with the Hive Mind, you can manage them. You
can get them to the treatment house. There are
other humans like you at Parthenon. They await
your arrival.

Wintu turned to look at Bear in the gleam of orange moonlight. Lord, he was gigantic!

Bear removed his white helmet, exposing his furry, Apsape head and enormous lenses. His antennae quivered, as a sonorous boom resonated through Wintu's head, his entire body buzzing with sound.

You asked to be a Beekeeper! You're above the Bee-
keeper grade now. A Hive Human is like an angel.
Please accept the bee's gift with honor!

Bear Boone rose straight up in front of the full moon. His body burst into a thousand bees and flew off into the velvet night.

The drone army raised up the new queen and carried her to a throne of white, royal jelly. Wenona ate continuously over the next few months. She grew a flamboyant abdomen covered in short, yellow fuzz. She became a grown woman-bee.

The Hive Mind became her entertainment as she waited for the birth of her first brood. It was alive with a cacophony of buzzes, toots and beeps. It spoke a universal language amongst the bee folk, playing an endless array of GPS directions, chemical signals, waggle dances and Sun worship.

Her favorite show was Friends of Apis Radio, where folks called in to talk to Doctor Jack. He liked to read from his late father's lab notes. The quotes from the great geneticist, Dr. Bingham Barnes, always made the Hive Mind light up.

From my father's lab notes. Apis was at the edge of the apocalypse for its genus. If the bees died, everything would go with them. The bee venom had proved to be the cure for humanity's personal apocalypse. The bees had been present in the laboratory in that sense. With a step in a different direction, they could become a life partner.

Wenona smiled and sipped propolis wine. She had heard the stories before. They were on an endless loop. She opened the pod window to let in the Sun's beams, watching the light shimmering on the neon, green pollen walls. The doctor continued reading from his father's lab notes.

Apis sapiens would not be ruled by an Earth sign, but by the sign of the Sun, the source of electromagnetism that influences the hypopharyngeal gland. When we refer to the Hive Mind, we mean the radio waves emitted by the Sun. A human is one organism on an isolated island; the honeybee belongs to the hive superorganism.

The Apis sapiens takes from both, being self-aware and group aware. The Hive Mind is a radio in its head.

A child's voice asked, *Doctor, are you a drone or a worker?*
I'm a worker, son.
How old are you, Doctor Jack? asked another.
Oh, I'm getting on in years. I don't like to say.

Wenona tapped her toes to the young Apsapes' synchronized Sun worship in the courtyard, their little feet stomping gaily, their fat bodies waggling, their golden crowns bowing to the Sun's glory and majesty. When she returned to the show, Doctor Jack was still reading from his father's lab notes. She sat and lifted her feet onto the soft bedding.

The sapiens form had the opposable thumb, the bipedal hip structure, large brain. The Apis form had superior communications systems, acculturation strategies, reproductive dominance. In the Apis, we had discovered the biological imperative humans had lost somewhere in the distant past. It would take a far shorter span of time to achieve population goals. It was an endgame scenario.

A child's voice asked, *how many children does the human queen produce, Doctor Jack?*
The doctor answered, *she gives birth to hundreds of Apsape babies in her lifetime.*

Wenona rubbed her belly. It began to jostle like elbows in a crowd. She shifted her weight. The humps and bulges rearranged; her belly flattened. There was a squishy noise. Slimy things began to flop out, googly eyes on roly-poly heads. The Apsape nurses swaddled each precious one, kissed its face, and held it up in the hive's window to greet the Sun.

In a month or two, they would become fur balls with long arms and legs. They would learn to walk. They would learn to dance. They would put on plays. They would tell jokes. They would build stuff. They would talk on the radio. They would live. That was the thing. They would live.

SPACE, THE FINAL INSULATION

Howard Hughes was in love with Nevada—it was a practically lawless state if you had the gears in place to work the system. He owned seven casinos in a state that allowed any other businessman to own only five. But there was one thing about Nevada he could neither abide nor change. That was the nuclear bomb tests. Howard believed the atoms being smashed in the desert permeated every underground nook, creeping silently into the drinking water. It was a source of constant distress, and he had desired to pay someone— maybe even President Nixon—to stop the tests.

Howard solved the problem another way. He left the Desert Inn in Las Vegas and moved to the Acapulco Princess Hotel in Acapulco, Mexico. He picked up the phone. "Can you get me some more Poland Springs water?" he asked Dean. "I only have a couple dozen left in here."

"Sure thing, boss."

Dean heard the rapping against the wall—the

sound he had one day figured out was the organization of business documents stacked around the perimeter of the room. Howard started with the ones on top, picked up a short stack of papers and tapped the four sides on the floor. He returned it to the top of the stack, then he tap-tap-tapped the whole stack against the wall seven times, counting: "1 2 3 4 5 6 7." If any pages were sticking out, he repeated the process. It took hours to go around the room creating symmetry in the stacks.

Howard did the same with the boxes of Kleenex tissues, except with these he counted the boxes again and again, making sure he got the same number each time. He repeated the process with the paper towels and the Poland Springs water. He stayed away from the collection of urine jars.

The furnishings and floor were covered in white sheets, and on the floor a path of paper towels on top of that—double insulation—led to the bathroom where, naked, he scrubbed the germs from his hands. He was naked because clothing was contaminated by supernatural association. He didn't want to supervise pants, or things in the pockets of pants, like money and its affinity with the ghostly particles of immorality. Howard didn't carry money. He had no idea how much money he had. His staff paid the bills.

Howard lived in awareness of quantum entanglement every second of every day. In his world, one particle of thought—a thoughtron—could affect another arbitrary point far away. When one thoughtron traveled out there and stuck on someone else's, it was defiled by association—the foul thought rubbed off on his, making his inner life unbearable. It created imagery he didn't want to see—perhaps an old sexual escapade with Sunny, a prostitute at a Nevada brothel. Or a memory of his mother's shameful berating as she bathed his private areas.

He isolated himself in his dark bedroom with the draperies taped to the wall at the edges, his movie projector looping the same films. This ritual kept his faculties entrained on repetitive dialogue, his thoughts boxed inside his head, not out there where the lures of sinners sparkled like syphilitic fireflies.

With the volume turned up loud, Howard's small room became an echo chamber trapping his thoughts from taking wing. The aviator who had once flown around the globe in record time was permanently grounded. He was watching his favorite movie, *Ice Station Zebra*, which starred Rock Hudson, Ernest Borgnine and Patrick McGoohan in a race to retrieve a fallen Soviet spy satellite from the North Pole. The satellite had taken pictures of sensitive U.S. defense facilities and had dropped down in the Arctic.

The Tigerfish nuclear submarine's mission was to beat the Russians to the British weather station. Prop Russian paratroopers landed on set. It wasn't as cold in the Arctic as we thought; nobody wore hats. After watching the movie so many times, though, Howard no longer noticed.

Neither did Rock Hudson.

Odd thing about it, Rock wasn't paying attention to the immediate calamity aboard the Tigerfish, which was taking on water and sinking fast. The star had begun a behavior that rattled Howard, because this was not how the story usually went. Rock began talking as if he knew Howard, as if he was concerned about Howard's predicament.

"What's eating you, man?" he asked. That's what Howard heard, but Rock's mouth was moving as though he was reciting one of Howard's favorite lines uttered by his character, James Ferraday: "We operate on a first name basis. My first name is Captain."

Howard was suspicious of anyone who spoke to him. There was only one man allowed to speak to him, and that was his personal aide, Dean. And, sporadically, his barber, Sam. He didn't respond. He was stretched out in supine position on his bed, naked and hardly moving. "Nothing bad can happen if I stay still," he muttered.

"That's insane, man," said Rock. "Completely bonkers. You need to get out of that bed before you get a big bedsore on your skinny rear end. Look at you. Do you even weigh a hundred pounds?"

Howard began to repeat the new dialogue. "Completely bonkers. Big bedsore. Completely bonkers. Big bedsore." These new lines made him anxious. He reverted to counting: "1 2 3 4 5 6 7."

Again, Rock intervened. "Listen Howard, help me understand why you're lying there utterly naked except for that long gray beard and stringy hair. Why, Howard?"

"Nothing bad can happen if I stay still," he whispered.

"How does that even work, man? Explain it to me."

Howard disliked having conversations with anybody. Period. But Rock Hudson wasn't just anybody. He responded, "well, if I went out there and bought some new clothes, I'd have to touch someone's hand, or touch the clothing that's been touched by someone's hand. That puts their guilt and shame on me. Or, I might have to sit in a chair another person sat in and be seduced by the atoms of their lust."

"I see your dilemma, buddy," Rock responded with empathy.

Howard hummed a deep resonant note that felt good in his chest. He kept it going for a time. He ate one more piece of chicken from his soup. The Campbell's people had already trimmed it to the exact size he needed, but it wasn't as hot as he liked it. He rang Dean. "Can you please heat my soup?"

Dean entered the bedroom with a Kleenex tissue in his hand. Howard wrapped the paper towel around the bowl and held it with a clean tissue. Double insulation. He had stopped the projector as Rock was giving him detailed instructions on how to escape the germs and radioactive voodoo of Earth. Dean took the bowl.

Howard flipped the switch and Rock resumed. "You're searching for a lawless place like Nevada, but even Nevada isn't good enough. What you want is a place where you can start out with a clean sheet of paper and build a community that would be exactly the way you think it ought to be."

Rock stopped and stared, his mouth agape as if the film was dragging. Howard flipped open the door of the projector, ready to adjust it with his long thumb nail. It wasn't stuck.

Rock's face turned meditative. If he thought any harder, he might burn a hole in the film. His expression smoothed out and he became animated. Almost giddy.

"By Jove, Mars is that place! But, you know, it's completely untamed. You'll have to start from scratch. Take some capable men up with you; take a city planner, a good chef, some strong able-bodied guys, and welcome their wives and children. Even their pets, darn it!"

It was true, the billionaire thought. He really was the only person alive who could start a Martian colony—the one with the technical savvy, the money, the impetus to escape the soul-sucking feds who accused him of siphoning billions of dollars in defense contracts.

It was ludicrous. He had done no such thing. Why were they always trying to nail him to the cross?

He had threatened the Senate committee, "I'll leave this country and never come back." And he had done exactly that. He had gone to the Bahamas, then to London, and now Acapulco, but he missed Las Vegas. He was a man without a home.

Howard began taking notes. What he was hearing was fantastic. He drew a line down the middle of the page as Rock suggested.

On the positive side he wrote, "No germs. No

taxes. No feds. No city officials. No Congress. No police."

On the negative side he wrote, "Pants."

It wasn't a bad tradeoff.

Rock went on. "There won't be any telephones. But you'll need something. You can improvise with empty soup cans. Have Dean wire those up. Take Jean and the kids up there with you. She's a trooper. The kids will love it. You can build a miniature golf course for them, a real fun kid's game."

Dean knocked and came in with the soup, heated for the sixth time that day. The boss was talking to himself as he scribbled in his writing pad. It sounded like he was saying, "Take Jean and the kids. She's a trooper." He passed Howard the soup bowl wrapped in a paper towel, a Kleenex tissue covering his hand. The boss took the bowl with a clean tissue from the box. Double insulation.

As Dean headed for the door, Howard stopped him. "Say, Dean. Do you remember how to make a phone out of soup cans and wire, like when you were a kid?"

"Sure do, Mr. Hughes," Dean smiled. "I made the best walkie-talkies."

"Could you make up a couple sets, one for me and you? A couple more sets for Jean and me and the kids? Plenty of line, huh, Dean?"

"Can do, boss." As Dean walked out and shut the door, a shudder of dismay ran through him. Howard and Jean had separated, somewhat amicably, and they sure as hell never had any children.

Howard awoke the next morning thinking about Rock Hudson's ingenious plan. He never knew Rock was such an educated man—delightful and innovative—a god damn good human being and patriot. He switched on the projector. As seawater sprayed into the sinking submarine, and Ernest Borgnine screamed like a girl, Rock ignored his surroundings and continued to counsel Howard.

"Space is your final insulation, my friend. Once you leave the heavy atmosphere of Earth, with the corrupting influence of three billion inhabitants," explained Rock, "your thoughtrons won't stick on anyone. They'll be dust in the solar squall. You'll be cured, man! Cured!"

Howard had never considered this solution to his mental difficulties, but Rock had a point. He'd make sure he took the movie with him—*Ice Station Zebra* would be his greatest source of inspiration. Rock Hudson would be "on the hook" now, meaning he'd be paid to be on standby. Howard never completely severed ties with anyone because they knew details about him the media would pay obscene money to hear. "Fire the son of a bitch," he'd say, "but keep him on the payroll." He had countless people on the hook—ex-girlfriends, doctors, a barber, a nurse— paid for their silence about Hughes; how long his hair was or whether he clipped his fingernails.

He put his ideas in a memorandum to be delivered to Rock. He came up with an attractive offering figure. It was muddled in intricate details—he needed to cover all his bases, and then some, to fend off his anxiety. The memo would be typed by his secretary wearing white gloves, then delivered by gloved hand to a cutout, a middleman, who would then get it to Rock Hudson. The world out there was a maelstrom of people who wanted to entrap the billionaire. He couldn't be too careful.

Howard and Rock began intensive sessions on the needs of the Martian colony. They discussed food, water, shelter, oxygen. Spacesuits for protection from radiation. "You can buy some spacesuits from NASA," Rock suggested. "The suits will recycle water from sweat, tears and urine. Take all those jars of urine you've been saving. You're already ahead of that game."

"When you get there, have your men build a huge ice dome to protect from solar radiation. Bring some seeds so you can grow vegetation for food. Bring up some fish for farming. You can recycle your poop for nitrogen."

Howard couldn't get over how brilliant the man was. A problem solver extraordinaire, Rock would be his co-pilot and right-hand man. He began work on architectural drawings for a dome built of shimmering ice.

Howard picked up the phone. "Dean, would you please get Sam in here for a haircut tomorrow?"

"Sure thing, boss."

"And how are those walkie-talkies coming along?"

"I already got started on them, Mr. Hughes."

Dean had shined up a dozen soup cans and

turned them upside down on his work table. He banged a nail clean through the bottom of each one. The boss wanted extra line, so he picked up a brand-new ball of kite string at the hardware store. He strung lots of line through each one and made extra-large knots so the string wouldn't fall through. He also made one three-way set in case the boss wanted to conference somebody in. He wondered why the boss was being so super secretive that he wanted to talk in cans. Or was he just off his rocker? Who knew with Mr. Hughes?

Dean completed his first set and tapped out his secret knock on Howard's door. "I've got a prototype talkie set for you to test."

"Come on in, Dean," Howard said, excitedly. The gleaming, silver cans were attached by red kite string. Dean handed them both to Howard for quality control inspection. Howard smiled broadly and handed one to Dean, saying, "Go in the bathroom with it, Dean. Let's try it out."

"How's the sound in there, Dean? Over and out." said Howard.

Dean replied, "I hear you crisp and clear. Over and out."

The next day Mr. Hughes returned the prototype cans with two pages of numbered modifications, and Dean got to work on the completed sets.

Howard dialed his wife, movie actress Jean Peters. Jean was a farm girl, a real down to earth type. She preferred roles she could really grab onto and understand on a deep level—not glam sirens, but real human beings mired in hardship. Through them she could realize her true self. She and Howard had a heart to heart talk. Something had changed in him, and she liked it.

A week later, Howard's aides transferred him to a stretcher and hoisted him over their heads, carrying him down nine flights on the outside fire escape of the Acapulco Princess Hotel. To any normal observer it would have looked as though the hotel was hastily removing a non-paying derelict in his bathrobe, but that guess would have been way off. He was the invisible man. The wealthiest man in the world. And it wasn't the first time his staff had exited him from a penthouse suite in this manner.

They spirited the boss into the back of a waiting van and raced to the airport. The two pilots of the hired aircraft were forced to stand a distance away so they could not see who was boarding.

When the plane landed in Los Angeles, they rushed Mr. Hughes to the hangar where the largest aircraft ever built was housed. Though it was known in the newspapers as the "Spruce Goose," Howard hated that name. Built almost entirely of birch wood veneer, its proper name was the H-4 Hercules—that was "H" for Hughes. He'd been contracted by the government to build three of them for the war, but due to his impractical embellishments he had only managed to build one. Nobody thought it would ever fly. Too big to get off the ground, they said.

The aides had purchased clothes for Howard; casual slacks, white shirts, a World War Two bomber's jacket and a brimmed Stetson hat. The old crew of the Hercules—whom he had kept on the hook all these years—had turned the flying boat into a Noah's Ark, of sorts. By the time Howard arrived, the behemoth seaplane was stuffed to the gills with men, women, children, pets, food, seeds, building materials, and all the essentials of a new colony. It was so massive it had to be pushed with its wings removed through the streets of Long Beach. The excited children aboard the Hercules grinned and waved out the windows to a forming crowd.

After reattaching the wings, the Hercules was launched down the ramp and into the harbor with 150,000 pounds of freight. It floated on the water like a feather. With its eight engines roaring, the Hercules picked up speed; three miles out on the choppy sea it hit ninety miles an hour.

"Put the flaps down fifteen degrees," Howard ordered his co-pilot, Captain Ferraday. That was a takeoff order. The flying boat took to the sky. Destination: Mars.

The H-4 Hercules was caught on radar as it soared over the ocean and left Earth's atmosphere. The world was stunned. Radar control reported the errant plane all the way up to the Commander in Chief. "That son of a bitch," said Richard Nixon.

The stewardess, Jean Peters, stood in front of the cabin. By this time everyone on board had been helped into an astronaut suit, and they were buckled into their seats by an elaborate harness assembly invented by Howard Hughes. Jean was suited up except for her helmet. Her hair and makeup were perfect.

"You must keep the helmet on at all times," Jean emphasized to the children. "If you must wee or poo, you can let that go where you are. It may feel a bit funny the first few times, but you will get used to it." The children laughed and said that was gross. "You shouldn't for any reason get out of your seat. Or take your helmet off," she repeated.

"I'll bring the food packets later and show you how to consume those. Your suit is hooked up to your vital signs, so we know exactly how you're doing. In a short time, we'll hit zero gravity and your magazines and books will begin to float. For your safety please pass those down the aisle so I can collect them and lock them up."

Jean glanced up. A small animal in a full astronaut suit came floating down the main aisle from the rear of the plane. Jean began her slow move toward the cargo hold where the pets were being held. She grabbed for the cat and it swatted her hand away, tumbling end to end in the new slow space-time. As more small pets floated overhead, the kids reached up and gave them a shove to get them whirling across the aisle. A gravity-free badminton game ensued, as dozens of cats and dogs, and one lizard, twirled around the Hercules cabin.

Right on cue the swashbuckler, Howard Hughes, made his entrance in a leather flight jacket and a dapper hat, smiling perfect teeth under his trim moustache. He hit his floor marks perfectly for the scene, raising his arm to catch a floating chihuahua.

The dashing Captain Ferraday stepped into the cabin behind him, his dark hair sticking up in the anti-gravity. Together Howard and his co-captain rounded up the pets and returned them to the caged area, which had not been properly locked. They were met with wild applause as they returned to the cockpit. Calamity averted.

Howard was back to himself. He invented a dome that allowed colonists to walk as if their weight was the same as it was on Earth. Built over a huge crater he named Zebra, the dome covered two hotels and two private bungalows. Inside the Desert Inn, he put a moving boardwalk that allowed colonists to stroll while looking at holographic Earth sights. Oh, yes, he invented 3D holograms. The Sands Hotel had a carnival of games for children and adults, including miniature golf. On the grounds was a full 18-hole golf course, with solar powered golf carts and paved roads in between lush green turf.

Mars Station Zebra had real telephones now, invented by Howard Hughes. The old soup can phones had a spot in the museum at the Desert Inn. On its monthly trips back to Earth, the Hercules crew secured patents at the patent office for all of Howard's inventions. The Hercules returned each month stuffed with supplies and people who had camped out in long lines to become colonists of Mars Station Zebra.

Howard and Jean lived together in one bungalow with their children; Edna was 6 and Jules was 4. Rock lived with his boyfriend Lee in the other bungalow. Howard had long ago lost the impulse to control his thoughts. Jean and he were as happy as clams. After they put the children to bed each evening, they dined at the Desert Inn Hotel.

"What are you doing in this movie?" Howard asked Jean across the table. "There are no women in *Ice Station Zebra*."

"This isn't *Ice Station Zebra*, Howard," Jean told him again. "This is our life—the best part I ever played."

"Right. I keep forgetting."

Jean smiled at the waiter and requested the farmed rainbow trout.

"Give me the fish too, Dean," said Howard.

Jean and the kids stood on the edge of the stage under the banner celebrating the tenth year of Mars Station Zebra. Howard spoke to the crowd gathered. "I thank you all for your courage and dedication over the past decade. Mars Station Zebra could never have made it without your enthusiastic spirit."

Then, Howard went off script. "I'd like to thank the Motion Picture Academy for this award for my picture *Two Arabian Knights*." The Hollywood crowd roared with applause.

The doctor was exasperated. "Why isn't this

man in the hospital? His kidneys are shutting down."

"He doesn't like hospitals," said Dean.

"Is that you, Dean?" Howard mumbled. "Give me the fish."

Dean went to him and took his hand.

"Where is Jean?" Howard asked.

"She's in the bungalow with the children."

"I'm glad to hear we're still married. And we've got kids now?"

"One of each, Howard. Your son is your spitting image."

"Good to know it, Dean. Thanks a lot for being here."

Howard smiled. His eyes closed on this world. On all worlds.

THE MANAGEMENT

The building was shaped like a boomerang, a six-story high rise. The round flower bed in the front and a wide driveway circling it made the street technically a cul-de-sac. Behind the building, a cobblestone walkway led to a large sitting area near the pond, where you could watch the Canada geese come sliding in on their landing pads whenever the hell they wanted. I didn't have their schedule. The loud, little bastards alerted everyone, believe you me.

I sat on the bench day after day where the short bus picked you up and dropped you off, but the elderly services bus hadn't been by in weeks. The Management had locked the office and exited the building. They were paranoid about the Virus.

The first memo from the Management said we should stay six feet from each other when we passed in the hallway or on the stairs. Not very many of us were able to do stairs. Only one person—and their dog —was allowed in each elevator at one time. The social room was locked up. No more TV or card games. You were to remain in lockdown in your two-room apartment and await the next memo.

The memo said the bag lunches would be dropped off at noon daily in the first-floor lobby, but there was never anything there. I called the number on the memo and left several messages. I finally figured someone was stealing the lunches, but I could never catch anyone in the act. Just like I couldn't catch the nark slipping the deranged memos under the door.

Every morning I awoke to a new memo. I had tried sleeping in a chair to catch the rotten fink who was doing it, but I fell asleep every time. The memos made it sound like the Management was there for us. They had our best interests at heart. Yeah. A hundred plus elderly and disabled tenants left alone with nobody running the office. Nobody answering the phones. Nobody filling the candy machine, the soda machine. No rides to the grocery store.

I was down to macaroni with ketchup. I took stock of my condiments. The ketchup was running low and I'd soon be eating catsup. This called for drastic measures.

I awoke with a start. Another memo slid halfway under the door. I opened the door quickly. There was nobody in the hallway. "Son of a bitch!" I read the memo carefully, looking for any nuance of actual concern from the Management.

Dear Residents: The current world public health

crisis is causing some people to become under-
standably anxious, depressed, angry, or to ex-
perience hard-to-manage emotions. We under-
stand how this quarantine could affect your
mental health. Being alone does not mean having
no one to talk to. Gavin Gray, substance abuse
coordinator, is available to answer your ques-
tions and direct you to counseling resources.
Please call—.

"Shit! Fuck 'em all! They've left us all here to die!" I peeked out the door. The hallway was clear. I needed to talk to Randy Baumgarten next door in 240. If he didn't answer, I'd try someone else.

I wrapped softly on his door. I heard him shamble up to the peephole. "Randy. I know you're in there. I gotta talk to you."

"We're not supposed to see each other socially, Merk. Didn't you get the memo?"

"I got the fuckin' memo, Randy. All the goddamn memos. Who's the snitch, Randy?"

"Stop talking so loud, Merk, for Chrissakes. I'll be right out."

In a minute I heard a shuffling sound and the door opened. He was visibly thinner than he'd been when we last played Poker. And back then he had no meat to work with. That was four Sundays ago, the day before the Management exited the building and left us on our own. Around when the short bus stopped swerving around the cul-de-sac, and the bag lunches became invisible, pink, zero-calorie designer totes. If you catch my drift.

Randy's gaunt face belied the terror he was living, alone in his apartment with only the TV for company, and an obtuse president making shit up as he went along. The lunatics were running the asylum.

"Have you tried calling the number on today's memo?" I asked him.

"Sure. I left my number at the beep," Randy said, coughing into his sleeve. "I told Gavin I need my prescriptions filled and I could use some food. And some clean water. The tap water smells foul and it's brown. I've been boiling it." He trailed off and hacked again into his sleeve. I thought I saw a trickle of blood.

"Have you got any food left in there?" I asked.

"I've got one can of ravioli I'm stretching out."

"How are your condiments holding out?" I had a plan brewing in the back of my mind.

"I've got some relish. I've got a can of tomato paste, half a jar of green olives. Might have some lime juice, if that's a condiment."

"Could be a condiment if it's mixed with something else."

"Interesting," he said.

I made a mental list of his condiment condition, as I heard the distinct pull of a bolt drawn into a lock. Conny Conroy from 241 peeked out slowly, her glasses tilted crazily on her nose. She stared for a few seconds with that poker face I'd seen many a time peering over an unreadable hand. Because that's what a poker face is. Then she shut the door.

"Conny," I asked as calmly as possible. "Are you

okay in there?" I took a couple of steps across the hall and got a whiff of shit. Conny was known to be a pants shitter. She was probably out of adult didies. I wrapped lightly on the door. "Conny, do you need anything?"

She slipped a note under the door. "Diapers. Water. Food. Someone to talk to."

I lost my shit at that point. "Fuck the Management!" I said to Randy. "They've left us here to starve to death. I'm invoking the Clown Posse Comitatus Act!"

A three-alarm fire zigzagged across Randy's face. And well it should have. It meant the neurons were firing across the bow. It meant he was alive. Even if he was dying of the Virus.

I went back to my apartment and rummaged through the bags in my closet. I pulled out the green, curly wig, the red nose, the orange checkered suit. It took much longer to find the big shoes and the oversized pocket watch, which were in the suitcase under the bed. The white shirt was dirty, but it would be covered by the roll-up tie. The troupe wouldn't be able to ignore the call to arms.

Within the hour, me and Randy were in the elevator—that's right—two of us, together, breaking the law, tearing it up like mental bozos. This morning's memo was taped to the elevator wall.

"Who the fuck is doing that?" I said.

"Nark!" Randy answered, beeping his red horn.

We got off on the third floor. I wasn't used to the clown shoes. I tripped a couple of times on the way to 311. Randy squirted his daisy flower prematurely. We were both a little rusty. I knocked quietly, listening for movement inside. There was nothing. Sheila should've been in there. I knocked louder. Still nothing.

We shambled over to 323. Arthur Clearwater was home. The news had traveled by phone. He opened the door wearing a huge red smile and a wife-beater shirt. With a playful wave of a buoyant white hanky, he let go of the dove inside. By 8:00 bedtime, we had a small clown troupe assigned to knock on more doors in the morning.

By 5 a.m., another memo had slid under the door. This one decreed the Clown Posse Comitatus Act a federal offense. It directed every member of the Westmeath Apartments Clown Posse to cease and desist any association with this outlaw group.

"Fuck 'em! Fuck 'em all!" This snitch had to die. I was feeling a mental health break, big time, and I wasn't planning to leave a message with Gavin Gray to refill my prescription. I was angry and loosey goosey at the same time. So, this was what it felt like being off my psyche meds!

The first business of the Westmeath Apartments Clown Posse was to feed people; to do that we needed to catch some small critters. We gathered up what we might need for the job. We had three nets large enough to catch an overweight Dachshund. There were two of those glutton mutts, incidentally, living in the building. In an abundance of caution, Hadwin Sands printed up a notice for the two elevators, warning people to keep their pets close by.

We gathered a collection of sharp implements we could use to poke the animals to death once they were inside the nets. "If we really put ourselves into that, it could be an effective tenderizer," I said to Arthur. He grinned and elbowed me in the gut. He was one of the few who liked my sick jokes.

Next, we cleaned the two outdoor grills and made sure we had enough gas. I wrote up a memo and slipped it under all the doors myself. This memo, I bet, was read with more interest than any of the others.

Dear Westmeath Apartments Friends. On Saturday at noon we will hold a cookout in the outside dining area. We will honor the six feet distance rule. One person per elevator. Please leave your dogs at home. Please bring condiments and any food you can spare to my apartment tonight. Thank you. — Merkurio Santos. Apartment 242.

On Thursday, we caught more than a dozen rabbits and six squirrels in the nets. It was a bloody mess.

On our night hunt, we caught two raccoons. Some people weren't sure we should eat those. On Friday, a twenty-pound, blabbering turkey was tenderized on sight. It was exhilarating.

Secretly, I sent word around the troupe to see if anyone had any guns. The cookout would be huge, and the nark would certainly be present. The feds could be called in. This might be the last hurrah for many of us, but we were ready to go down with a sublime clown fight. Surprisingly, there were a number of hunting firearms hidden in the building. We had a few Mossberg Patriot rifles. Inexpensive, but they do the job. A featherweight Winchester. Nice little long-range baby. There was a Ruger American in the mix, and some real antiques from the Second World War.

On Friday afternoon, we got the news from Sheila's best friend, Bridget Donelan, that Sheila had died during the night from the Virus. Here was her note.

Dear Friends, my last wish is for my friends to grill and eat my body for Saturday's cookout. Please let me have the vicarious joy of being there. I love you all. — Sheila Dunphy, 311.

My little Sheila bo-beila! What a sense of humor. We had loved and lost and never loved again. I arrived at 5:00 p.m. with the wheelbarrow. Her body was light. The memos said I couldn't touch my own face, but I touched her cheek and said goodbye.

Bridget checked the soda machine and bought the last can of Coke. "Makes a good tenderizer," she said. I swore to myself, then, nobody would ever hear a tenderizer joke uttered from my lips.

Me and Bridget dug out a pit on the lawn and built a spit out of a broken umbrella stand. In the darkness we shaved Sheila's head. She had the lumps and bumps of a lifetime with an alcoholic husband. We pushed the spit into her bum and out her mouth. The last insult to a fine woman. I kept telling myself she wanted it this way. "Her dying wish," I said out loud, without realizing it.

Bridget glanced at me over Sheila's supine body as she rubbed her skin with Himalayan pink salt and Coca-Cola. The corner of Bridget's mouth twitched, but she held it together. We covered Sheila in aluminum foil, so she was unrecognizable to the others. The birds of spring tweeted home to young ones awaiting stories of the great raptors in pursuit. It was the same bedtime story every night. I squirted lighter fluid on the coals and started the pit turning. Arthur took the first shift at the Shaft. That was what we called it after that. Me and him, anyway.

I slept in the chair near the door and around midnight I heard something slide under. It was a small plastic prayer card with a picture of Saint Corona, the patron saint of epidemic diseases. I opened the door quickly and saw Agnes Doolittle shuffling away on her walker. She was wearing her white face mask. I walked up to her. "Agnes," I said, as I approached her as coolly as possible. "Are you the one slipping the memos under the doors?"

"I certainly am not," she replied. "I'm praying for your pathetic soul for being forced to roast a wonderful human being for a gathering of ungrateful assholes. But I'm not above it. I'll be there. Those are the sins we commit when we're hungry enough. God forgive all our souls."

I fell back to sleep and dreamed the vultures would be unleashed upon us, their beaks pecking wildly at my old, wrinkled face. I awoke with a start. Another memo! I ran to the door and opened it.

Gavin Gray himself! A puny, shrunken, statist who had never had a friend in the world, whose only dream had been to become a social worker so he could sit on dire phone messages while people died. Gavin turned to run, but I grabbed him by his pencil neck and pulled him inside, making sure to slam his forehead solidly into the door jamb. As he fainted, he let out a froth of air from his sick lungs. He had the Virus too.

I plopped him into a kitchen chair and got some rope from the closet. Working quickly before he came to, I tied his hands behind his back and then tied him to the chair with another length of rope. I thought of washing my hands with soap like the memos said, but I knew we were all infected with the Virus now. We were weak, little wrens who would never fly again. Unless I could get my plan in motion.

I called Arthur. He was the fat, rockin robin. He still had some meat on his bones. "Arthur. Come to my apartment now. Can you bring the wheelbarrow?"

"Sure, Merk. I'll see you in a minute."

Gavin had just aroused when Arthur stepped into the kitchen. "Is this the nark?"

"This is the nark, all right. I caught him in the act," I said.

"I ain't no nark," said Gavin. "I'm just doing my job."

"If your job is to spy on people, to sit on people's messages, steal their lunches, don't get their meds, don't bring them water, you're a nark." I taped Gavin's mouth with silver duct tape and gave him a fierce clout between the eyes with my favorite hammer named Maxwell. That would shut him up for the ride.

We blasted out the door. It was 2 a.m. The hallway was quiet. The lights flickered in the ugly wall sconces. I was sick of the shitty carpet that hadn't been cleaned in decades; the grim, beige, institutional walls that hadn't been painted in years. We were fresh out of hope, out of claw, and out of condiments. Somehow you just know when your time has come, when desperation is the only phone number in your book. When F.U. is the only station on the dial.

Arthur hit the elevator button. We laughed about the tenderizer joke. Okay. I said I wouldn't laugh about that in honor of my Sheila bo-beila, but my word is shit.

Chapelle Benedetti was spinning the Shaft. I

called out to him in warning, mostly so I wouldn't get my own head knocked off. "Hey, Chap, it's me, Merk. I'm with Arthur. We've got the nark."

Chapelle's white eyes stood out against his dark skin. He was Italian and Cajun, a serious fellow, who took an interest in our hog-tied package. Gavin was awake and fighting against the ropes. Chapelle was a big guy, known to be a brooder, a lone drinker who had just finished a bottle of Daniels. He walked over to Gavin in the half moonlight. "I never figured it would be anyone other than this piece of shit, who wanted to be a shrink but could never do nothing but lick his mama's underwear."

Chapelle gave Gavin a backhand across the mouth with a sound that cracked in the crisp, night air. Gavin snorted blood out of his nose. "Ain't you the fella supposed to give us the bag lunches?" he asked, as he bent Gavin's fingers backward. Gavin whimpered behind the duct tape.

"Where are all those bag lunches?" I asked Gavin. I could barely understand him as I locked his nuts in my vice grip, but I thought he said number 433. I dug into his pants pocket for his keys and threw them to Arthur. "Would you please do us the honor?"

While we waited for Arthur, we broke every one of Gavin's fingers with an enormous rock from the pit, and then broke his arms by lifting him backward off the ground. The sound of his bones snapping was pleasing to my ears. His moaning, though, was off-putting.

"Christ, quit the griping, you chicken shit!" I

bashed him in the ear with Maxwell. We stripped
him naked and had him watch as Chapelle continued
roasting Sheila. He made a pathetic mewling sound
deep in his throat.

Arthur returned with the news that Gavin had
hundreds of bag lunches stashed away. Not only that.
He had boxes of candy, chips, and peanuts; cartons of
7-Up, Sprite, Coke, Snapple. He had it all.

"We're gonna have a swell cookout tomorrow,"
Arthur said.

"Oh, we sure are," I said. "Let's wake Bridget."

As the sun peeked over the eastern seaboard,
me and Bridget shoved a pointed umbrella stick up
Gavin's ass. The rod made crunching sounds as it hit
gristle on the way. He wailed like a snitch. It accidentally poked out between his ribs and we backed it up
and straightened out the concourse. Bridget rubbed
him with salt and a couple cans of Coke from his stash.
We wrapped him in foil.

Sheila's alarm went off. She was cooked. We
began roasting Gavin slowly on the Shaft. His cries
sizzled from inside the burnt foil; his flesh smelled
like bitter remorse. I wouldn't plate that beef for my
worst enemies; nark meat wasn't fit to be served at
any party I'd put on.

At 11:30 Saturday, the elevators started moving up and down. The Clown Posse had spread
the food tables out at a distance and lined chairs

along the hedges. Some people arrived in their own motorized wheelchairs, and we arranged them in a circle so they could talk to each other—what little they'd have to say over the body of their dear friend Sheila, roasted in the last can of Coca-Cola. Instead, what they found surprised everyone. Piles of sandwiches, mystery meats, potato salad, vegetables, chips, candy, condiments, soda, juice and booze. This was more food than anyone had eaten in a damn long time.

At high noon, Frank Borelli stepped out of the back lobby into the sunshine with his beautiful Ruger. Gaeton Zaino scurried past him with his Browning Stalker. I pointed to the east corner of the building and touched my red clown nose. Gaeton touched his. His eyebrows were edged in black, his mouth painted white and edged in red. He wore an oversized, flowered suit, with hilarious short pants. A bright orange Afro.

Over the walkie talkie, Chapelle reported he and Fritz Wallentin and four other Clown Posse Members had the front cul-de-sac covered from behind the trees. The Posse was in position. Six in front, six in back.

Me and Arthur performed our old skits while pouring rum and cokes. Some guests could barely eat, like Randy, coughing up the contagious sputum of the Virus. But they drank. Everyone was drinking that day—there are no alcoholics in foxholes. There are plenty of pants shitters, though, and Conny was there. Others too. Not to just point her out.

Arthur pulled doves out of his pants to no end of hilarity. Guests began to dig into the mountains of meat and sandwiches. It was a delightful afternoon. Sheila was the hit of the party, as she would've been in life. "Tender" was the word on the wind, and nobody was shy about it. Someone started a sign-up sheet and passed it around. If I recall correctly, it was titled "Delicious in Death." Maybe they weren't such assholes after all.

Just as the raptors began chasing the bluejays to their nests, the feds pulled up in front of the building. Chapelle buzzed me. "Mercenaries. I'm counting eight Humvees. Loaded." I heard the jabber of AK-47s out for some elderly bloodsport and the crack of hunting rifles returning fire from behind the pines. I heard Chapelle scream "Live free or die, motherfucker!" before his voice went dead. That bastard had some moxie.

Mercenaries sprinted through and around the building like rabid monkeys. I saw Frank fall first, hit in his sad, clown head with the spray of a semi-automatic rifle. Arthur was beside me, blasting with his antique British infantry weapon. The next time I looked over, he was turned into bloody mincemeat right where he stood in his rubber clown shoes. I shot one of those mooks in the brain with my M1 Carbine. I was suddenly back in Nam. I picked out another one. "Live free or die, motherfucker!"

The guests began screaming; I'd like to say they ran, but they were feeble, elderly people with the Virus, unable to get away from the vultures that came out of the sky next. Sniper bullets rained down from green, army helicopters until every single resident lay dead on the ground bathed in blood. Except me.

That was around when I got the shot to my shoulder that sent me flying ass over tea kettle over the shrubbery. The building blew high into the sky at the same time. I had opened the gas lines and waited for the feds to work their magic, give all my people a spectacular ride home. I was the only one who saw the magnificent visage—drunk, little cardinals flying with their faces to the sun.

I laid there dying until the final cleanup, when a female infantry discovered me on the ground and ordered me removed to the hospital, where I spent two months recovering from the Virus.

I'm now fed pen inmate number 007-F.U., Merkurio Santos (the newspapers called me the grim reaper clown). I'm very much alive and back on my meds. Come and visit any time. Just make sure you haven't got a dove in your pants. And no tenderizer jokes, eh?

THE HORROR AT INNSMOUTH HIGH

The antiquated elevator shivered on its ropes while the irritable Broscoe stared into my face, one bulging eye wandering nervously on the periphery. I waited while he strove to string together a sentence hinting at the source of his hostility. Finally, with those long drawn out vowels peculiar to North Shore inhabitants, he came out with it.

"This exact same thing happened thirteen years ago," he said, "except back then news didn't travel so fast, so we didn't have no newspaper people like yourself come up here nosin' around."

"Really, Broscoe? Is that what you think I'm doing—nosing around?" I replied.

He was an unusually tall, thin man with an elongated head, receding chin and thick, blubbery lips. His worn, wool jacket covered a wrinkled dress shirt. "Call me Broscoe," he had said, as we shook hands at the entrance to the school.

"You can call me Ruthie," I replied.

I had departed for Innsmouth after breakfast on assignment from the *Miskatonic Valley Mirror* to gather some juicy tidbits on the "pregnancy pact" between seventeen girls at the Massachusetts school. I felt a tremble in his hand which I attributed to the drink—I know some things will drive you there, and this decrepit school building crawling with young ruffians was clearly one of those things.

The bell rang, classroom doors flew open, and a sea of pimply juvenile delinquents dashed out, slamming into each other and bopping each other on the head with their books. When the way was clear, Broscoe ushered me through a narrow hallway to the elevator.

"My office is this way," he said.

After a stretch of silence in the elevator, I knew it was up to me to keep the conversation going with the ill-tempered administrator. "So, what happened at Innsmouth High thirteen years ago?"

"Welp," he said, and stopped again to string his story together. "Back then, it was twelve girls pregnant at the same time. This year, it's seventeen. Every thirteen years since I been here, we have a slew of pregnancies."

"But was there a pregnancy pact, Broscoe?" I responded, as I scribbled the numbers in my notebook. I deigned the interview to have begun now that my subject was suddenly talkative, but he wasn't answering questions so much as going off on his own tirade.

"They like to call it baby bump syndrome," he replied. "It's got a cute ring to it for the magazines.

Ain't nothin cute about seventeen youngsters in the school pregnant at the same time. It makes the place bonkers."

"I imagine that's quite true, Broscoe, but was there a pregnancy pact that you know of?"

Again, he ignored the question. I was beginning to get a sense for why he was as peeved as he was, having to waste administrative time on a mushrooming public relations disaster. I became apprehensive in the confined space and began to wonder why the elevator was taking so long to travel one floor. To my relief, it abruptly slammed to its destination. Broscoe pulled open the cage-like doors to the ancient carriage.

"So how long have you been the Principal of Innsmouth High?" I shouted over the blasted machinery noise. Broscoe didn't answer. *He probably didn't hear me*, I thought. When I was a kid, I hated school basements; usually the teachers brought the whole classroom to the restrooms together, and for good reason. All the clanging and banging made our imaginations run wild.

I followed Broscoe down a long corridor with sooty, behemoth furnaces standing along the left side. These, the source of the infernal noise, were leaking profusely and throwing off a thick, roiling mist. This was the outer wall of the building, but I noted there were no windows along the upper wall to shed even a glint of sunlight. Only a few dusty bulbs hung from the ceiling to illuminate the way, and most of the bulbs had gone out. Water leaked from the furnaces, pooling into brown puddles along the pathway.

Broscoe moved in a long, shambling gait through his familiar scape, as I picked my way carefully over the wet, uneven cement. Finally, quite a distance ahead of me, he stopped and looked back, and by a trick of lighting I fancied he was sprouting gangly protuberances from his face.

"Oh, come on, Ruthie," I muttered. "Seriously?"

Down we dropped. The water began to seep into my shoes. I became disoriented in the damnable dark cavern, where the angles of the walls and ceilings suddenly made no sense, where nebulous shadow movements seemed to reconstruct the building's very footprint. The stone architecture here was fascinating—where could the immense, green stones in this grotto have originated? Their shapes and sizes, their exquisite disposition imposed upon an impossible geometry, was a thing of stupendous beauty.

Placing my open palms on one of the dank stones, I felt the rusting hinges of my mind open to an acute awareness of a distant chronology, one that human contemplation alone could not fathom. I had the sense I was initiating an intelligible communion with the mysterious creators of this place. An eldritch, alien mind seemed to telepath to me alone, to breach and pervade my psyche, to blend the language and culture of our distant races; they —the Great Ones, as they called themselves—their croaking speech seeming to wash over a babbling brook, and I—Ruth Dunbarton—student journalist, now Earth Ambassador, rapt in wonder.

Broscoe had disappeared ahead of me and I was oddly unconcerned. My mind was captured by extraordinary vistas of a watery, alien homeland, dense glades and marshes where creatures frolicked—living things imbued with a variety of curious shapes and sizes, protrusions, knobs, antennae, fins, horns, buttons, tails and untold exotica. Some were chunky and square, splashing with a guttural ha-ha-ha!; others sylph-like, only to be seen in their squirting movements from here to there.

An otter-like thing zipped around with a little motor on its behind, a series of gills fluttering quickly enough to propel it fantastically before me. A flat, polymorphous shape rose high and resplendent above me, squealing in euphoric delight as it splashed through me. Peculiar birds took wing above the inlets and fjords, calling out to each other on the soft-hued horizon, where two setting suns cast colors barely imaginable and utterly unnamable.

At last, my gaze set upon the golden spires of a hidden conurbation just below the sunset to my left, and I thought I heard the rumbling of immense waterfalls that churned the life of an underground city. Lord have Mercy. These were the things of opium dreams, and I cared not to let them go.

A hollow thrumming stole my reverie; it was the furnace kicking in. I jerked my head toward it and took a step on a surprise incline. I tripped and dropped my notebook into a puddle, my cell phone crashing to the cement floor. I bent to pick it up and the screen lit with a text alert from the Principal of Innsmouth High, Mr. Broscoe. He wrote, "Hello, Miss Dunbarton. I wonder if you got lost. I'm waiting for you in my office on the second floor."

Terror gripped my heart—to what frightful end had I been waylaid while my mind gave way to fruitless phantasms? I turned to go back to the elevator. As I took the first feeble step in the dark, my right ankle was lashed with a rubbery, lasso-like thing that started to wind its way grotesquely up my leg. Immediately, then, my left ankle was lashed in similar fashion so that I was immobilized. I decided my best course of action was to quickly return the message to the real Broscoe. I typed, "lost in base ...." and then gave way to the terrible ordeal that followed.

The slimy appendages dragged me by the ankles along the cement floor, scraping whatever skin wasn't covered by my dress. I bumped along on what soon became a dirt floor, screaming obscenities, until a strike on the head silenced my cries. I thus, thankfully, missed the next events which brought me to be tied to a cold slab, surrounded by a naked cast of amphibious figures chanting in an unidentifiable tongue.

A loathsome, humanoid silhouette with an octopus head and numerous, disgusting, feelers entered my drugged vision at the entrance to the cave, each wriggling tentacle under its own autonomous command. I was overpowered with the fetid reek of rotting fish. The cultists became animated with frenzied dancing as their hideous, hybrid god ceremoniously mounted me, the sharp claws on its hands and feet threatening mutilation. As it perched above me, its wingspan filling my frame, it stared into my face and spoke in a bestial babel somewhere between croaking and barking.

All around me the minions of this monster frothed forth a jumble of gibberish, which culminated in cries of, "Cthulhu fhtagn!" It was then that I squeezed my eyes shut and sang a children's song before I again lost consciousness.

I awakened in the hospital in an addled state and requested a young nurse to inform me as to my whereabouts, clutching her sleeve in a grip stronger than she imagined I would have, considering my feeble condition. She pried my obstinate fingers from her clothing and bolted from the room, returning with the doctor, who pushed me back into the bed—I had one leg out and was on the verge of toppling out. I begged to know what type of accident had befallen me. Agitated and unable to comprehend my situation, a tranquilizer introduced me once again into the sweet arms of oblivion.

Screaming in horror, I awoke in the night not knowing where or who I was. I soon discovered I had been transferred to the Miskatonic Psychiatric Hospital. I still had no remembrance of what had happened. I recalled placing my hands on the cool, green stone, but my recollection ended there.

During my lengthy convalescence at the psychiatric facility, I was further exploited by freely administered Valium and hypnotism. My psychiatrist, Dr. Mordecai, made repeated attempts to release the contents held fast in my mind's grip. I refused to indulge the primary event, to push past the bizarre communion with the stone, but that alone was enough to impugn my mental state. During my hypnotic sessions, I began to channel the alien race who had installed the transmission device in the subbasement of Innsmouth High. Dr. Mordecai was fascinated by my description of the frog-faced beings who spoke in a burbling language while gathered around a black crystal sphere. He increased my Valium dosage and urged my parents to lengthen my stay.

Each monotonous day blurred into the next. Strung along the walls of the cafeteria, red, pointed leaves became insipid snowflake cutouts. One day, an ornamental fly buzzed in my ear, "hmmmm, hmmmf?" It asked if I would take joy in its dessert. It revolved its yellow, plastic tray so I could remove the cake. It said its name was Martin, and it asked my name in return. "Ruthie," I told it, unsure if the sound I made was my name, or if my name was the sound I heard.

My ongoing lunch chatter with Martin was uncomplicated. I began to find my way out of my drugged stupor, to find footholds in the dizzying cliffs of madness. We spoke of what we might do when we returned to our lives, the feasibilities and hypotheticals such a return could encompass. No longer dumb to temporality, no longer stranded in a boat with no oars, our souls opened up to the flow of life's infinite stream. On a blustery, December day, my parents came to take me home. As Martin hugged my shoulders warmly, he passed me his card. It read, "Martin Chauncy Freeborn, Attorney-at-Large."

Taking maternity leave from the *Miskatonic Valley Mirror*, I began to write in my journal daily for my own peace of mind, to see if a new clue might come to light about that accursed day.

Martin and I filed a lawsuit against the Town of Innsmouth alleging grievous bodily injury and rape, which occurred in a subterranean dungeon under Innsmouth High. The Principal, Mr. Broscoe, claimed to have found me roaming the basement, fully clothed and coherent, shortly after he received my text. He maintained I wasn't missing long enough for the events described to have taken place, and he insisted nobody who works there, or who has ever worked there, could possibly fit my description of the other Mr. Broscoe.

The jurors who visited the school saw nothing out of the ordinary in the basement, which they described as well-lit and dry. Martin hired a satanic cult research group to search for the sub-basement tunnels, but their digging has not yet revealed the hidden catacombs. The Innsmouth School District hired one of the best Boston lawyers, who sent a settlement offer from which Martin read to me the following trash talk:

> *Your client's claim to have been raped by a scaly cephalopod named "Cthulhu" in the non-existent watery dungeons of Innsmouth High*

is a ludicrous confabulation. I can prove that her story is embellished almost word for word with the chimerical fancies of Rhode Island's State Birdbrain, Mr. Howard Phillips Lovecraft, which flourish on the internet like hair on a chia pet. If you don't shut down this obscene publicity stunt, my client, the Innsmouth School District, will have your client committed for observation at the state asylum for the criminally insane.

The lawyer informed us the school district intended to countersue for malicious defamation, unless I was willing to do two things: (1) admit that my misadventure may have been the result of a "regrettable mixture of certain prescribed medications," and (2) advise my "two-bit fake archaeologists" to abandon all attempts at unearthing the site.

In the end, Martin and I accepted the $1.5 million-dollar settlement offer, along with the stipulated conditions. We were married in a quick ceremony at Arkham City Hall. We purchased an aged but handsome estate on the shore at Innsmouth, Massachusetts, where at sunset the croaking frogs call out to their kind from the marshes beyond the white cliffs, and I can almost comprehend.

On our first tour of the home, the workers at the sprawling estate showed us a passageway leading to rooms beyond walls hastily put up to conceal discovery—dusty rooms laden with fascinating curios and heirlooms of a distinguished Innsmouth mariner family. Roaming the rooms on my own, I came upon an antiquated painting of a frog-faced individual, round-orbed, staring with that errant eye that seemed to inquire deep within.

As I gazed into its bulbous orbs, I realized it resembled the same Broscoe who stole me to the basement of Innsmouth High. Terrified, I screamed inarticulate phrases mixed with a familiar children's song before I fainted, crashing headlong on the floor below the amphibious naval officer's portrait. Martin at once advised the construction crew in their own common language to reconstruct the wall with the best masonry they could find, threatening a lawsuit if they ever discussed the hidden rooms with anyone.

My Martin runs in respectable circles and, although I have fully recalled the entire, detestable incident at Innsmouth High School, I have not shared the shameful details with him. I am disinclined to perplex him with haunting thoughts that should just as well remain concealed, for he worries so about me in my fragile condition.

Martin has hired a midwife named Imelda, a hoary relic from the town of Innsmouth with a cavernous, rotting mouth, who follows with glee his every admonition for my supposed safety. She disallows my roaming about the house when my husband is taking clients in his law library, locking me in the bedroom to knit coverlets and rompers for the baby. Imelda brews me distasteful herbal teas of anchovy and bitter rockweed, insisting these ingredients will feed the infant's favorable predilections.

The seventeen pregnant Innsmouth High girls have all given birth to healthy babies. I have several pen pals among them who claim to have been virgins prior, as was I before the harrowing event. The "Innsmouth 17" all refused to join me in a class action suit to strengthen our cause, because their parents believed their fascination with my "implausible chronicle" was unhealthy. However, my communiques with the girls have uncovered some curious aberrations to which I have also been privy.

My young pen pals have disclosed recurrent dream imagery of an undersea stone palace and a leviathan who lies dreaming there in the primordial city of R'lyeh. I will admit to no one that I experience these psychic emanations nightly, wherein I float over His sleeping form in a watery villa, and He opens one eye in recognition of me.

I am swallowed up in that moment by that eye and carried to a time in which my ancestors roamed these walls and spoke of the future after the dreaming, when the very rumblings of the ocean's mantle would recite the incantations of the awakening.

I see giants rising out of the sea, green scales shimmering in the moonlight, their blubbery-lipped mouths working in silent song, their webbed pads squishing on the road with the rhythm of a soldiered band. "They are coming," I say to Martin, as I rise and pace the creaking floors of our bedroom. I rush to the window and shout, wild-eyed, "The tides are issuing forth the Great Ones. They are coming for me! For me, Martin! Do you hear me? They are coming for their queen!"

Martin shakes my shoulders and throws cold water in my face, shouting, "Stop this madness, Ruth!"

As he rings for Imelda, he administers another vial of laudanum under my tongue, as prescribed by that maleficent Dr. Mordecai. I can smell Imelda coming with the cold-pressed pickerel oil, with which she grotesquely caresses my growing mound while singing in the olden tongue to my unborn bairn.

As I slip under, I replay Cthulhu's words in the dark dungeon before He took me, by His earthling proxy, as his wife; where He promised me that when the stars are right, His city shall rise from the ocean, He shall revive his loyal subjects, and I shall sit at His side for His Most Righteous Reign.

SEE?

"**S**tay home!" blared the TV.

I wish I had listened.

I had been out of the house once.
Just the once.

Something grabbed hold of the car
crumpled the roof,
with a shriek
and a whoosh of wings.

It guided the car in a loving bubble
floating it down,
noiselessly,
into the Hockomock Swamp.

Pterodactyls swooped and tore at piles of stink.

Disco music floated on the thick air.

From a tin hut out yonder
        the Hobbamock
spirit of death and disease
        screeched my name
            and bade me enter.

Its gigantic claws shredded my dress
        It took me in its beak
        and we flew over mountains of trash
rising dizzily into the cliffs
        where monstrous and deafening
            dwelled its own kind.

    It dropped me into its nest,
    naked and squirming,
levitating
    above cavernous
                wide open
                        mouths.

    See?

        See what happens when you leave the house?

25 HELLO

They sang "New York, New York" in drunken choruses until the new year arrived with a bang and a fizzle. About an hour into 1985, Ed and Darcy Shannon crowded into an elevator with their waggish new friends. With a loud snap, the elevator lurched to the right, piling the partygoers onto each other—and they fell ninety stories in a shrill, unified scream.

The elevator plunged deep into the sub-sub-sub-basement and slammed into the Mesozoic layers, finally coming to a stop. The Shannons peeled their bloody bone bags off the people beneath them and began the distasteful task of separating who from who in the packed chariot.

With everyone's parts straightened out, the genitals being the most queried, the spirits drifted up through the Earth's layers. Ed Shannon, playing the tour guide, chattered on about the dinosaurs buried in the layers; the ten-ton T Rex and the small-brained Stegosaurus. They hit the hard mantle and the crusty snow, and the blaring sounds of New York's streets denser than any of that. In front of Macy's on West 34th, they all bid each other a good eternity, the drenched sadness of loss no longer the province of their gone souls. Ed and Darcy set their spectral beams toward the heavens and followed the stars home.

The Shannons wandered the Afterworld Kingdom for a decade of Earth time, taking counsel from many a spirit traveler about where they were supposed to be and when to be there, but Ed could never get on the stick. He told the baloney story about the dinosaurs so often Darcy started to believe they had really seen them.

They stopped in a friendly town called La-Gloria, where Ed became the Outreach Manager of the Minotaur Museum; everyone agreed the handle "part man, part bull" seemed fitting. After another decade of Earth time, they ventured on to Hosanna's Cove to ogle the mermaids. Darcy put her foot down on Ed's designs to become the Outreach Manager there.

All along, a discomforting feeling gnawed at Darcy. Her spirit had diminished to a low spark, as if she were moving away from her primal energy source. Ed seemed happy enough with his new spirit life, but Darcy missed her children, especially her little girl, Claire.

One day the answer arrived in a Holoid advertisement blinking over Eternity Pass. It flashed in all Earth languages:

> *25 Hello! Your contact haven. Talk to your family today! At Eve's Den Gaming Mall in Paradise City.*

At Darcy's urging, they arrived in a few days at the busy gaming mall. They checked the floor plan for 25Hello and floated into the cool air-conditioned store.

The attractive arachnid behind the desk told the Shannons that Hello was the best contact game in the business. She pulled down a map behind her with all the locations highlighted. "Hello has an influential presence in Paradise City, and 25Hello is our 25th store," she said as she pointed to their location. "Our representatives will take care of all contact services." The Shannons joined right away.

Claire Shannon affixed the top layer of the cake to the thickly frosted bottom. Her hands were chunky and pale, steady and sure. She spread the cream frosting luxuriously on top and all over the sides, then she said in her little girl voice, "We'll surprise Daddy when he comes home."

Mama said Daddy wouldn't be home tonight. He was working his other job. We will eat all the cake, then, me and you, said Claire. She cut two thick slices. Claire talked about the dance in two weeks. Could she get a dress with polka dots? She sure could. Could she have pink fingernails? Only the lightest pink. Could she wear lipstick? She certainly could not, and she should stop asking.

She stuffed herself with cake until the doorbell chimed. Wiping her hands on her apron, Claire wobbled to the front door, her forward momentum impaired by her side to side gait. She had grown as round as a ball, and she didn't give a whit what the doctors said.

She pushed her wiry, brown hair off her forehead and put one eye up to the peephole. "Mama. Come here," she said, in her little girl voice. "It's a wispy black woman with a powder blue coat and a matching hat like the Queen of England. She's got a polite, pink smile. I think she's a Jehovah's Witness."

Mama always said to be kind. Claire opened the door, and the lady vaporized and condensed near the floral print sofa. She turned to Claire and said, "I am Miss Irving from 25Hello. I have a message from your parents."

Over a cup of tea, Miss Irving told Claire her parents were gladdened by this opportunity to communicate. Tears rained down Claire's face and her lower lip trembled. "My parents died when I was ten years old. I pictured them riding the elevator up and down, unable to get off. They were looking for us. I baked cakes and waited for them to come home. I thought you might be them."

"I see a steeple with no bell, an empty vessel standing in for your heart," said Miss Irving. "Your loss will be filled by the one who will cross the divide."

Claire stared into Miss Irving's faint gray eyes. She wished she knew what all this meant.

Miss Irving told Claire all she needed on her end was a Ouija board and her two brothers, Mitch and Jordy. It would all come together when they got there, she promised. The instant Claire paid the connection fee and signed the 25Hello Contact Agreement, Miss Irving disappeared, leaving only her teacup and wrung-out teabag. Claire called Jordy first. He was the empathetic one, the kind one. A lot like Daddy.

Jordy was mystified. "So, she disappeared just like that? You're sure she was there?" he asked. "The teabag was wrung out. That could be a sign. Um-huh. She was dressed like the Queen. Um-huh. Claire, I just don't see how all this happened."

The little girl voice came out then—the sad, whimpering contrivance she had used as a child had been perfected as an adult.

"Now, Claire, don't cry. I didn't say it didn't happen. I'm just saying, it's weird. But, let's do it here. I'll borrow a Ouija board." They set the game for Friday night at Jordy's apartment in South Boston.

Her younger brother Mitch was more cynical. "Come on, Claire, this didn't happen," he said. "She rang the bell? Why didn't she float through the door? Christ almighty! You gave her how much money?"

Claire wept, "Mama and Daddy want to speak to all three of us. Mama will be sad if little Mitchie isn't there."

"Here we go! Permission to land the wing nut!" said Mitch, taking a belt of whiskey from his silver flask. That high-pitched whining always on the heels of wanting her way—there was a genius in there under the layers of subterfuge. He relented. "I'll go but I'm not staying for the crybaby shitshow when this stunt comes undone."

Right on time, Claire rang the buzzer at Jordy's dark doorstep. The address was always difficult to find, being buried into a side street, boxed into someone's back yard, and hidden in the basement. To add to this difficulty, there was but a sliver of a moon, and the lights in the apartment had gone out.

Jordy came to the door with a flashlight. His dark, shaggy mane fell in waves across his eyes, his shirt was worn and dirty, and he had a couple of front teeth missing. "The electricity went out an hour ago," he said. "I found some candles. I've lit all I could find."

"Didn't you pay your electric bill?" she giggled, following him inside. The room was aglow in candlelight, throwing dark shadows of all sizes and shapes onto the walls. "It looks lovely," Claire said, as she set about filling the water glasses on the table.

Presently, Mitch rang the buzzer. It had started raining. His jacket was soaked through, and his usually spiked, blue hair was plastered to the sides of his head. In the pitch dark, he stumbled on the stairs. And he wasn't alone. He had found a way to turn a private family tragedy into a date with someone he had just met at a bar. Marisol Adams was petite, fortyish, her graying hair pulled into an upswept hairstyle. She had told Mitch she could speak to the dead. That was all he needed to hear.

Marisol took over. She began to rearrange the room, placing several candles on the sideboard around a picture of Ed and Darcy Shannon. She advised them on how to use the Ouija board, and she volunteered to jot down the messages from the spirit plane. "Do not put too much weight on the planchette. Let it move by itself. Does anyone have a childhood memory to establish the identity of the spirits?"

Mitch, being the youngest, didn't remember much, but he had one oddly enduring memory: dad's frozen pants. In the winter Mom would take them in from the clothesline, flat and crunchy. The way she danced around the kitchen with them was the funniest thing in the world to young Mitch. "I've got one," he said.

"Go ahead, Mitch," said Marisol.

"Mom, do you remember how you danced around the kitchen with Dad's frozen pants?"

On the other side, Darcy tried to smile, but couldn't remember after so many years of not using her lips. She answered, "yes, I remember the frozen pants." But what came through a minute or two later was something different.

With their fingers held lightly on the planchette in the shadows of the dimly lit room, they awaited a reply. Finally, the planchette began moving, at first faltering, but then speeding up its response from Darcy Shannon. Marisol read aloud exactly what the board had spelled out. "Reform yourself whiskey drunkard."

Mrs. Shannon was shocked by the false answer, but it wasn't her fault. Mitch, his face pallid, reached for the whiskey flask in his back pocket.

Together, the siblings searched Marisol's face. This wasn't Mom. Claire's turn was next. She fought the tears beginning to sting her eyes. She didn't want to share her private memories with someone other than her parents. She now recalled a part of the 25Hello Contact Agreement that covered something called "common derelicts of the wires." Miss Irving had seemed to hurry over that part.

"What if," Claire asked, "there's someone else on our private connection? Is that possible?"

Marisol touched her hand, whispering, "I'll take this." She stood and commanded loudly, "To whom are we speaking tonight? Please identify yourself."

The board was quiet for some time, and finally the planchette began moving. It spelled out: "I am Arcus Pluvius—I am Perception. I am Chitta Raum—I am Revelation."

As Dad jokes go, this one's a doozy, thought Jordy. But it wasn't a Dad joke. On the other side, Darcy was floating upside-down with her hands at her throat, and Ed was attempting to reach her. The professionals at 25Hello had shut down the game and were applying first aid.

The group made room for Marisol at the round table. "I suspect you've got a demon in your game connection," she said. She clenched her fists and shouted, "this entity is a foolhardy piece of fluff that thinks it has permission to run afoul of the rules of psychic communication!"

All the lights switched on and every electrical appliance began running: the microwave hummed, the mixer whizzed, the blender whirred, the telephone rang, and the radio thrashed speed metal. "It's talking to us," said Marisol. She stood and paced nervously. "A demon can run interference on every line in your house, including radio frequency, telephone wires and electrical wires."

The razzle of a drill screamed from the ceiling, and a giant tube descended slowly to the floor. A vessel sped down the tube and landed with a thwap. Out of the vessel, in a cloud of vapor, stepped a most peculiar person. In one exaggerated hand gesture, he silenced the infernal house noise and snapped out his business card.

"My name is Vanth Jarta. Thank you for helping to make 'Hello' a household verb."

All eyes failed to blink. Rising forward uneasily, Jordy accepted Vanth's business card. He checked it and passed it to Mitch, who studied the tube, the card, and again the tube. It did not compute. Mitch passed the card to Claire, whose lower jaw had not found the upper as she passed the card to Marisol, who read it and leered up, way-way up, at Vanth.

He was nearly seven feet tall, his bald head tracked with stitches. He wore a black, brocade tailcoat with wide cuffs, and a white ascot tied under the collar of his white shirt. The dress code at 25Hello was strict: No vampire capes or fake teeth.

Jordy nervously got a chair and a glass of water for Vanth, who joined them at the table. His face was crowded. There was nowhere to land. He had first a substratum of burnt, puckered skin overlaid with inflamed pocks and pustules. Sinewy stitches pulled together what was once a nose. His left ear was situated lower than the other and clipped, or perhaps bitten, jaggedly at the bottom. Grayish purple bruises ringed his eyes. On the left side of his mouth, an untalented morgue technician had taken a tuck, which created a drooling pocket of slime that looked like a second mouth.

He asked them to describe the problem. Marisol spoke up nervously. "I believe there are one or more demons interfering with the connection."

Vanth was quite interested in the new person at the table. "Do you work for someone, Marisol?" asked Vanth. When he spoke, his second mouth dribbled thick liquid. Just then, his troubled ear slid down to his collar. He slapped it and pocketed it like a lost button. The vacant spot was bloodless.

"I work only for myself," Marisol replied, and looked away in revulsion.

"Let me explain who I am and what I do," said Vanth. "I am a communications specialist from 25Hello. It's sometimes hard for us to help you from our side, so we send someone out to fix the problem from this side."

He smiled widely, revealing pointed, rotting teeth. His foul breath drifted across the table like a plague-ridden fog, an odd mix of cow cakes and formaldehyde. "I'm not only responsible for guiding the dead to the afterlife, but for their continued happiness and sanity while there." He pounded the table. "Bah!" he exploded in a ridiculous laugh, sending spittle into the air. "I've been told I look like the ferryman on the River Styx. But nope. That is my third cousin. Not me!"

God damn crazy person, thought Mitch.

Claire shuddered. Was it pity or revulsion? Now her mind was fueled, running through possibilities. His distant relative was widely known for guiding humans through the dark tunnels of the afterlife. She had read about that hero. Was Charon the name? A man from this distinguished lineage would have to know the answer. He must tell us. But what if the answer was bad?

She crushed her rising apprehension. Pushed it down. She cleared her throat. It came out as a squeak. She cleared her throat again. She had everyone's attention. It came out in her little girl voice, "Are Daddy and Mama in heaven or hell?"

Vanth cast a somber glance slowly at each person. "Let me be the one to tell you, dear children of Ed and Darcy Shannon, with considerate regard for your feelings."

Claire gasped and Jordy reached for her hand.

Inhaling, Vanth rattled as though he did not breathe air, but sucked water through a single gill. "There is no such thing as heaven or hell. The Afterlife Kingdom is strictly based on the gaming contact experience." He pushed his chair back and stood tall, so they had to crane their necks. "If your loved ones are forgotten, cut off from you, their souls wander aimlessly, kept hostage in a bleak, soulless, artificial intelligence."

Vanth skulked around the table. A frigid wind sent fingers of ice outward toward warmth. He passed Jordy, walking directly to Claire. She shivered visibly when he stopped behind her, touching the back of her chair. The skin on her neck crackled like ice on a pond. Claire fought the urge to turn and look up, or else she might propel her dinner all over the table at the sight.

Vanth continued wetly, "those souls who have dwindling access to communication are cut off, and they wander in mad circles like your parents are doing. As they move out to the edges of the game, they will become the property of the AI, and they will be declared incommunicado!"

"Incommunicado from what, exactly?" asked Mitch, with derision. "When you die you go into a game? What kind of masochistic game is this?"

Vanth advanced toward Mitch, a crease of petulance folding his brow. "Let me be candid, sir. Your parents have wandered dangerously into the shadows of the AI due to Ed's bullshit stories, moving them farther away from the activity, indeed the sanity, of the gaming mall."

He drew a cloth from his pocket to wipe the dribble from his second mouth, and he continued. "Ed seems bent on tweaking the world to fit his narrative, but he is stalling in a danger zone that could close in!

Target him!

Grab him!

Torture him for eternity, for it knows no time!" He paused for emphasis. "And the AI will be happy to pull in your mother and play with her like a cat plays with a mouse!"

Vanth swept his arm across the top of Mitch's head, unleashing a horde of large, sharp-toothed, clacking termites from his armpit. Without a cape, much of the effect was lost, but his thespian shouting made up for that. "They must remain in Paradise!" he roared. "Do not let them wander back into the desolation of the AI where they will become unreachable."

Vanth walked to the middle of the room, where he poised for perfect theater. "Hell is not a place," he yelled. "It's a condition!"

He took out a bronze astrolabe and rotated the gears to the death date of Ed and Darcy Shannon: 1:18-1985. The ancient device began to chatter with the haunting cries and ephemeral whispers of the dead. Images bounded out of the tube and into the room. A slew of malformed ghouls jigged around the table, pointing at their genitals with filthy hand signals. A sleazy fiend with a rotting piehole stuck its tongue nearly into Claire's ear, one bloodshot eye on the side of its head oozing stinking liquid. Claire recoiled and gagged behind her hand.

Vanth stabbed the ugly creep with a pin, and it popped out of the room. "Please ignore those devils," he said calmly. "They are replication errors that have been stuck in the Hello game for centuries. If you give them attention, they replicate further."

He dialed the astrolabe and found an open passage into the heavily trafficked game. The door to the tube opened with a swoosh. Vanth stood inside the vessel; the termites and the devils followed like pets, and they disappeared together into the ceiling.

Claire lifted her chunky arms onto the table and flopped her head onto them, sobbing. She was terrified to learn of her parents' close call with the AI in the Kingdom's lawless outback. She stamped her feet and banged on the table with her fists. Her little girl voice was garbled by tears and snots. "If we can't find Mama and Daddy, I'm gonna die. I want my Mama. Want her. Want Mama. Want her. Want Mama."

Marisol grabbed some tissues and touched Claire's hand gently. Claire raised her head and took the tissues. Tears soaked her face and dripped from her top lip to her quivering bottom lip and dribbled into the creases of her double chin. She wiped her face and blew her nose.

"Don't cry, Claire," Jordy said. "Vanth will find them. He's kicking ass. Listen to him up there!"

Vanth's vulgar swearing was within earshot as he subdued the Hello game entities. The clash of swords and bloodcurdling screams rent the air. He shouted "Hello!" as he daggered each one. The clock on the wall ticked. Claire visited the bathroom. The clock on the wall tocked. More shrieks of "Hello!" and lewd language came from the ceiling. Jordy filled the water glasses. The clock on the wall tocked. Mitch swigged from his flask. He glanced at Marisol. The clock on the wall ticked. He was starting to think about cocktails with his new lady friend, but with a thwap and a thunk, Vanth landed and stepped out of the tube in a cloud of fog.

"Just as I supposed," he said, as he took his seat, "your game connection was mucked up with demons of every suit and stripe, every domain, from aerial liars to terrestrial fire starters. Just atrocious." He slurped on his glass of water with both hideous mouths.

Vanth did some calculations and wrote up a receipt. "What I found in your connection was this: One extreme electrical demon, which shot out tongues of fire and burnt my coat. I'm sure you heard my embarrassing screams. Another one, an ancient and terrible terrestrial shit named Arcus Pluvius, was a childhood friend of Vlad the Impaler. Good to get that pile of bile banned from the game for eternity. And a mischievous, deadly egregore named Chitta Raum, who grew from an impish gallstone. Exceedingly rare. Believe it or not."

He placed his invoice in the middle of the table. "I have cleared out all hooligans large and small, and I request payment in cash of five hundred dollars."

"What?" yelled Mitch, rising from the table with his fists clenched. "Claire, haven't you already paid this crook?"

Vanth cut in. "My personal services are entirely separate from the contact agreement."

"Never mind," Jordy said. "He earned it."

Mitch grabbed the receipt and read it. "You've

charged us for losing your ear that fell off while you were flirting! You didn't lose that in a sword fight!"

Vanth grinned and asked, "Would you like me to go back up there and let those ghouls back in?"

They gathered up the cash and placed it on the table. "Wait!" said Jordy. "Can we get proof the connection is cleared?"

Vanth placed a tin transmog on the table; inside of it a small disk spun around. The carrier wave, which was transmogrified from the spirit plane, turned the disk. He tuned the dial, slowly phasing in the signal to a fine pinpoint. Claire perked up when she heard the familiar voice. The sound was airy; yet, in a few seconds recognizable as her dad's voice, his manner of speaking, and his tenor when he was outraged.

"This is a scam!" said the wavering voice of Ed Shannon. "Look what you've done to my wife! Now I must carry her. I certainly hope this disability isn't permanent!"

The 25Hello representative who spoke next sounded familiar to Claire. It was Miss Irving. "Mr. Shannon, please don't leave. Your wife is under medical supervision, and the farther you take her outside Paradise City the less attention she will get. Your lines are cleared now. Your children are waiting to talk."

There was no stopping Ed Shannon. From the sound of it, he heaved Darcy over his shoulder and slammed the door behind him. Vanth flashed a look at Marisol as he stuffed the cash into the transmog. He stood and pivoted, rushing for the tube. He opened the door and stepped into the vessel, motioning toward Marisol. She zipped in behind him. With a whoosh of steam, they were sucked up instantly into the spirit world.

Claire, Jordy and Mitch stared in a despondent daze. Jordy broke the silence. "So, did Dad just take Mom back out into the AI, which is basically Hell? He's about to make her really dead. Is that the correct placeholder here?"

"She's been dead for twenty-five years, Jordy," said Mitch. "I don't get how she can be more dead than dead."

"But you heard Vanth!" Claire whined, her face contorted with grief. "They'll become unreachable if they leave Paradise City. We were supposed to keep them there, safe from that AI monster, whatever it is."

"Not exactly our fault," Mitch replied, sarcastically.

"Do you really have to be such a shit?" said Jordy.

"Hey, look," said Claire, wiping her tears. "Marisol forgot her purse." She lumbered over and inspected her wallet. "Holy god, guys. She's a 25Hello consultant."

"Where did you say you met her, you idiot?" Jordy asked.

"Look at the door on the tube," said Mitch, avoiding Jordy's glare. "It just clicked open."

A blue light flickered from inside. Claire toddled over to the tube and peered into it. "It looks like a pneumatic tube like the bank has at the drive-through," she yelled, with her head inside it. "I betcha it works by suction each way. Or compressed air pushing the canister through." She squeezed her ample body into the vessel. Her little girl voice echoed. "No buttons either. I'll bet this tube goes one place and one place only!"

"No, Claire. Stay out of there!" Mitch yelled. Before either of them could reach the tube, the door snapped shut and she disappeared with a thwap of suction.

Claire stepped out into a world of bland, beige sameness, like a painting of a sandstorm. The stark silence asked no questions and gave no answers. Once you'd gotten accustomed to it, you wouldn't notice you were in a world that didn't speak. You wouldn't notice you were in a world without time. You wouldn't notice you were an artifact of an artifact.

Although she could see nothing, she heard footsteps running, first from the left, then from the right. She walked a few paces and was knocked flat on her ass by some kind of two-headed monster. When the dust cleared, she was looking at her dad—a thinner, frightful semblance of him—but still that lovable oaf, Ed Shannon.

"What are you doing here, dear?" he asked. "Wait till your mother sees you."

Darcy was lying across Ed's legs, and he began slapping her on the back with his gaunt hand. "Wake up, Darcy dear. Wait till you see who's here!"

"Daddy," Claire said. "where are you taking her? You mustn't force her to travel. She isn't well." Claire now had her small, ten-year-old body. She looked down in amazement.

The desert sand blew across Ed's skeletal face and stuck to his eye sockets. "Aw, she'll be okay, Princess." His teeth clacked shut. He touched her shoulder with a bony finger.

"No, she won't, Daddy. She needs to stay in Paradise City, or the AI monster will get her. Please take her back to the gaming mall."

"Did that ugly swindler say that?" Ed's voice rose in anger. "There's no AI monster. Those gamers are all cons, the whole mess of them. By the way, how much money did they fleece out of you?"

"Well, okay Daddy, you got me there," Claire admitted. "But where are you bringing her? She needs a power source right away."

"Well, how about you, Princess? You're her power source. Help me sit her up."

Ed leaned Darcy up against his chest. Claire rubbed her mom's emaciated face with her hands, calling her, "Mama! Mama, wake up!"

Momentarily, Darcy's eyes opened as she heard her little girl's voice. In all the worlds inside of worlds, this was her power source. Her little girl. Her lips, what were left of them, remembered and spread into a gigantic smile. Darcy hugged her mom. "I've missed you so much, Mama."

Back at Jordy's place, the brothers circled the tube, opened the door and called Claire's name up into the blue light.

"She's not coming back," Mitch said, after a time. He reached for his jacket.

"Where are you going?" Jordy asked. "You can't leave now. I have to call the cops."

"Right now?"

"Claire is gone, and I've got this . . . this, giant, pneumatic tube in my dining room. This is our only explanation for her being gone. Otherwise, we've got . . ."

"Police problems," answered Mitch. The light in the tube flickered from blue to pink, and a rush of vapor shot out of the bottom. "It's leaving!" he yelled.

The brothers squished into the vessel and ascended with a thwap. All that was left of their parlor game was a Ouija board and a purse belonging to an employee of 25Hello at Eve's Den Gaming Mall in Paradise City.

Darcy was up and walking on her withered sticks. The boys ran toward her in the blowing sand, and she hugged them passionately with everything she had.

Ed said, "Let's get in a huddle. We're a family again!"

"What's up, Dad!" said eight-year-old Mitch.

"What do you do for excitement around here,

Dad?" asked twelve-year-old Jordy.

"Lots of stuff! There's a great Minotaur Museum over in the outback," said Dad, excitedly. "I bet I can get my old job back."

As the family huddled, an unseen thing cast a massive shadow in the distance over Eternity Pass. The giant eye of an ancient watcher powered on.

It blinked in its own measured time.

It was not eager. It could wait.

THE MAINSPLAIN

Bombay Brown stared at the description of the playboy star traveler, Tamor Bleeb, until both eyes went west. His update was due on the FriendishNow dating site by end of day, or his boss, Tetanus Mercury, would pour hot, bubbling, whelk cheese down the back of his shirt. That stuff scars badly once the skin dries up. It could take weeks. In the meantime, let's just say, very unsightly when he goes bomping on the wriggley floor.

The colossal, angry mollusk, Tetanus Mercury, waved a large, threatening tentacle at Bombay's head. Tamor Bleeb had been a client for almost a century, the boss said. This would be a simple update, he said. Bombay ought to be able to handle it, he said.

Bombay re-read the particulars of the client's chart. He exhaled loudly. He whistled. He flopped his appendages over the desk, moved the pencils to the back, pushed some salt fish wrappers into the bunghole and turned the calendar to today's "Stab Calendar Joke." It wasn't funny.

The updated scores had come in this morning while Bombay was flirting with the new girl at the brine cooler. Now it was getting on lunchtime, and he had nothing. "Wake up!" He slapped his huge, conical head briskly, leaving a couple of suction cup marks. *Let's read what I've got so far*, he thought.

> *Tamor Bleeb, age 199, is a 61-Cygni Starship Admiral. Bleeb is a King-type on the evolutionary scale. He exhibits a powerful body, raw animal machismo, high intelligence. His home star, 61-Cygni, is a spectral, K-type, red dwarf in a binary star system, which is known to be stable for 20 to 70 billion years. K-type stars emit little ultraviolet radiation and no flares. Ladies, we are talking about an old soul in a handsome, young body. Admiral Bleeb is a Type 1, Reformer; principled, idealistic, ethical, organized and perfectionistic.*

That was a good start. Good solid start, Bombay thought. But he wrote that thirty krakles ago and hadn't come up with anything since. His workmate, Zelly, toodled him for the third time on his Pocketsplain. Bombay raised one of his eight appendages and pushed the squirt button. At the other end, his friend's eyes were sprayed with black ink. That would delay lunch while Zelly crawled blindly to the cleaning department.

Bombay told himself there would be no bucket of silver shiners or any bowls of yummy, creamy, whelk cheese until he matched up this playboy star traveler with a female in his soul class, preferably with a double-ranjee mating score. It was the only way to make up for his minus-net production last week. Mr. Mercury would treat him to an extra salt fish or two in his pay, and he would perform his weekly, molten whelk cheese torture on someone else.

Bombay went back to the personality page and wrote: "Tamor Bleeb flaunts the 'Type 6, Loyalist' pedigree: a hard-working, responsible and trustworthy type." That was good. "Trustworthy" was good.

Admiral Bleeb's updated picture revealed a large-eyed entity that stared blankly under a shaggy mop of hair. The admiral had a putty-white face and a short, angry sneer. He appeared slender and aristocratic in a constricted military uniform. Two rows of shiny, gold buttons added the wow factor.

But what was all the binging on the Pocketsplain? Can't a squid work in peace around here? "Inkstorm!" he tooted. Admiral Bleeb's new test scores were in. "Our test results show Bleeb to be a menacing Type 8, known to be challenging, aggressive and controlling."

"Ouch," said Bombay, "That could take some points off." He perspired saltily under all eight armpits. Either the office temperature was turned up too high, or his anxious thoughts of Tetanus Mercury's whelk cheese torture were becoming dreadfully graphic.

Wait! There was something else. Tamor Bleeb was being flagged on FriendishNow's private Mainsplain. The report said Admiral Bleeb had been a regular traveler on the trade routes between Alpha Centauri-A and 26-Draconis, which required long rest stops at the mid-point. There was some tomfoolery with the locals, and a police unit had been dispatched. There was a popular base camp there somewhere, Bombay recalled from his classes at Flipper's Travel School.

He checked the tellie logs—there had been a call for Tamor Bleeb about fifty years ago. The call originated from a planet called Earth. Bombay didn't have access to the message.

His research on the Pocketsplain showed Earth had been ensouled by two intelligent species, one aquatic and one biped simian. A third intelligent species was a group soul or hive mind. The Pocketsplain showed a picture of this planet: a blue sphere surrounded by white, whelk cheese puffs. "Inkstorm!" Bombay whistled. "This is the place!"

Bombay was so involved in the story of Earth, he jumped at the knock on his office door. He knew it would be Zelly standing on the other side with red-ringed eyes. He opened the door. It was worse than bad. There was no excuse for that type of behavior toward such a fine friend.

"Let's go for a bucket," Bombay said. "I'm buying." There was no apology though because squids will be squids.

Zelly worked in FriendishNow's records department. His job was to flag bad actors, and he had flagged Tamor Bleeb after reviewing layers of hidden materials in the company's Mainsplain. "Tamor Bleeb's arrest charges were kidnapping and impersonation of a foreign officer," Zelly said, as they sqwiddled into the Clams-n-More.

"Inkstorm!" said Bombay. They grabbed two barstools and signaled to the fair sea maiden behind the bar. "Hey, Sheenaw! A bucket of silver shiners, two big bowls of whelk cheese and two Salty Brines."

Bombay returned to his Pocketsplain and read out loud:

> The Earthlings had chosen to ensoul as the Warrior type. They chose a simian body—with opposable thumbs, binocular vision, omnivorous digestion and a large brain—in order to support exploration and warfare. Another intelligent species became ensouled as a water creature, in order to avoid the murderous behavior of the simian overlords.

"Smart move," they said in unison, as they pushed the live fishes into their tiny, squid mouths.

A bearded fella at the bar wearing a casual, striped shirt and a head bandana watched them with interest in the mirror. He sent over two Salty Brines and a bowl of whelk cheese. They waved in thanks. All the Televidgets in the bar played "Stalking the Wild Whelk," where monstrous, lumpy, dragon fish hulked invisibly in rock dens waiting to grab helpless pink whelk, who shrieked in terror while they were pummeled into delicious cheese.

Zelly read from the Mainsplain. "It says here, the Earth simian became an intelligent species millions of years ago, at about the same time as six others within ten light years. Several starships visited Earth from Alpha Centauri-A, Tau Ceti, Zeta Reticuli and 61-Cygni to welcome this ensouled race to galactic membership."

"I've got that in my Pocketsplain too," said Bombay. "It says their response was entirely fear-based and unwelcoming. They knocked them right out of the sky, killed them and took several prisoners. This happened in a place called Roswell-1947."

Zelly was equally curious about the message for Tamor Bleeb. He searched the star guide system on the Mainsplain for a history on the Earth species. It revealed a binary star system with one G-class star and a distant red dwarf on a widely elliptical orbit. The distant binary didn't swing around often enough for the inhabitants to know about it. It says here:

> *The highly-developed earthling civilization had been studied by various space travelers, who noted the planet was in constant warfare resulting in cyclically high death rates.*

"Did they ever become space travelers?" asked Bombay.

"Negative on manned space travel," Zelly answered, "but not all ensouled beings become technological, and not all technological beings conduct space travel. That's just a simple fact, but there's something odd here."

Zelly read aloud from deep layers of the Mainsplain:

Their technological prowess was alarming in light of their tribalistic patterns of warfare. On finding this aggressive species was interested in space travel, an ensouled group of galactic signatories had joined together to find ways to keep them bound to the Earth. The group was nicknamed the Babysitters.

Zelly slapped the keys. "I wonder what the jinx that means? It says here the furthest they got was their moon, once, on which it was discovered another group had already settled the 'dark side'. They never went back."

"Oh good, while I've got you there, what's the name of their moon?" asked Bombay. He sucked in a couple more silver shiners with his Salty Brine; it was good and salty.

"They don't have a name for it. It's just moon," replied Zelly. "But ancient myths say it's made of whelk cheese. The Earth has clouds of white whelk cheese and oceans of Salty Brine, with fishes large and small teaming within!"

"What a place! We should take a trip there." They slapped their arms together and merged their suction cups. They were so buzzed on whelk cheese they forgot the time. "Mmmmm," they said in unison.

"I remember there was a base or starship port around there," said Bombay. "See anything about that?"

Zelly flipped through even deeper layers of the Mainsplain. "It looks like the Earth's moon is a popular destination. Aside from that base on the moon, there are scads of starships parked in the libration points, which are points between two large bodies where a smaller object will maintain a stable position."

"Inkstorm!" said Bombay. The friendly guy at the bar sent over two more mugs of whelk cheese, and the two FriendishNow employees never noticed the time flying by.

"Here's something weird, said Zelly. He read aloud.

Earthling lives were so short and brutal, many of them had no time to evolve to a higher consciousness. As a result, they had to reincarnate through revolving doors to pay karmic debt. There were layers of ghosts spinning in a circular ring surrounding the planet.

Zelly whistled while he poked around in the Mainsplain. It says here:

Several highly-evolved Avatar beings had been

ensouled on Earth to guide them into peaceful galactic membership.

"What happened to them?" asked Bombay, a ring of pink whelk cheese spreading around his mouth. Zelly read.

The Avatars hadn't conformed to expected religious and societal norms and were executed. This delayed earthling soul development by thousands of years, leaving the species stuck on the planet with free will and nowhere to go. The unstable nature of its climate sent the civilization into shocks and restarts, slowing growth of intelligence, technology and higher ensoulment.

"Inkstorm! Cruel fate." said Bombay. He flapped at Sheenaw for a bucket and two more brines. "So, what about the message for Admiral Bleeb?" he asked. "Did you find anything about that?"

"Inkstorm! I'm trying," responded Zelly. "I keep slamming up against a wall. It seems like the wall was put there by Bleeb himself, which means he got the message but didn't want anyone else to access it."

"Why didn't he just delete it?"

"Clients aren't allowed to delete anything from the Mainsplain." Zelly took a mondo slug of Salty Brine. "I'm trying to unlock the message. It's from Earth, date-stamped 1965. That has no meaning to me. Let me try an older password."

Just then, in the large mirror behind the bar, Bombay spied Tetanus Mercury entering the Clams-n-More, surrounded by a rowdy mob of FriendishNow employees. He appeared to be carrying a bucket of steaming whelk cheese. Bombay laid his head on the bar, covering it with several arms.

"He's right there, Mr. Mercury," said the fella on the corner of the bar.

"Thanks, Admiral Bleeb. I appreciate your call."

Zelly slapped the keyboard of his Pocketsplain with his suction-cupped appendages. "Inkstorm! It's opening." He whistled. "I've got the message. I don't understand what it means."

Bombay uttered a muffled response, "Please. Just tell me what it says before he gets here."

Zelly read the message.

It's Betty Hill from New Hampshire, you fiend! I bet you didn't think I could find you with that stupid star map.

The scorching whelk cheese slid down Bombay's back and burned like the hot Hell he'd read about on the Mainsplain. The FriendishNow employees laughed loud and hard, and louder and harder. Zelly stood by with an ice-cold bucket of brine, ready to cool off his friend. Because that's what friendish friends are for.

SCREAM OF CONSCIOUSNESS

You think I'm just a dumb bed sheet tap-dancing with my tomahawk for the people in the front parlor? No! I remember how I got here. I was at the top of the ladder reaching for the jar of sweets, and in a lickety-split I was on the floor with my neck twisted and my tongue hanging out. Doctor Goodwin took one look and covered me up. He called the meat wagon to take me to his secret little morgue in the basement. That's where I am now, in the Gingerbread House mansion with the Bonetti sisters and the swell doctor.

My name is Pauline. At my funeral, my step-mother cried alligator tears over my casket. Even though she was all dolled up, I could tell she was zozzled. I knew she had wanted me out of her bonnet for a long time so she could tighten the screws on Daddy. I looked straight up her rummy nose and winked an eye. Just one eye. Nice and slow. She ran out the front door as fast as her getaway sticks could take her.

Bonetti's dressmaking shop is the bee's knees.

Miss Greta and her sister Viola make the loveliest glad rags for the hoity toity crowd from Providence to Fall River to New York. The second floor is the hen coop where the ladies try on dresses. On my first day, I followed Greta as she showed off shimmering bolts of silk and chiffon, and glitzy beadwork that spins noodles at swanky parties. I was touching the swell, warm velvets and picking up spools of handmade lace, as the Italian seamstresses peddled their sewing machines on the floor above.

I'll admit I was hypnotized. I was imagining myself floating in chic, palmetto green silk; then I was up to my broken neck in gas blue chiffon. I was matching it with a smart handbag and a cloche hat. I didn't mean to give her a fright. It was just a little sneeze from the dust, but Greta went sailing out of her brown, button-up shoes. Later that night, she made me promise not to make that noise behind her like a shout puppet or an Indian bassoon. It scares the daylights out of her rickety-sharp, and she might swallow some of those pins she has stuck out of her lips.

On my third day, I heard Greta in her phonus balonus saleslady voice on the second-floor landing. I ran back around the kitchen and through the front hall and looked up. She was gassing with two Flappers who had a dress fitting, a Ritz showcase and her daughter, a looker with a jet-black bob. I put my broken bum on the bannister and rode it up to get my peepers on the pair. They were no rubes; they were dressed to the nines. The little doll's name was Serena.

I wanted badly to play marbles with Serena, but just getting near her gave her a fright wig and a box of toads in her belly. She came apart at the seams and flopped to the floor. Nuts! Viola got out the smelling salts. When Serena came around, with my face right up to hers, she smiled like everything was copacetic. Later, I told Greta I hadn't meant to give Serena the willies, but she sent me to my turret to think about my mimsy behavior.

Greta is a sensitive, they say, and she can see me. Not like the dull visitors to the seances in the front parlor, where later that night I clomped by in my clunkers and blew my horn, making the heavy crimson draperies blow in ripples. Then, I stomped and dragged my loud chains like Jacob Marley. Some scattered, screeching, while others held their heads and wept, thinking I was their dearly departed. Again, Greta threw an ing-bing and sent me to the turret.

The next morning, Sunday, Greta held an ice-pack to her forehead. She said I was dreadfully hopped up for a little ghost girl, but she had promised me an ectoplasm praeline. So, I took the elevator up to play in the turret with my Noah's Ark and my marbles. My turret is where I'm happiest, with my spinning top, my doll, and my window. I had parked the Ark and let the animals out to see the show. We were looking out the window at the great big world, the greatest show on Earth. I was spinning my top on the windowsill near my little wooden pets, stirring up a woozy typhoon.

We were a sullen sight, all of us together under that mackerel sky over Broadway. Below, ladies under umbrellas twirled away the afternoon to the distant plunk of Greta's piano keys. I'd tried to get their attention before, but this time, It. Really. Happened! They looked up. One by one. The first lady to see me pointed and hollered, "What's that in the window?" I put my hands over my ears and opened my mouth big and menacing, and I screamed a scream of consciousness so real I scared myself.

I noticed that bear cat, Serena, who was carrying a swell, little bohunk doll. She looked up at me. Then an old gent came along. Then it was the copper who was directing traffic. That's when I pulled my noodle in from the window and got ready for the door chimes. I put my pets back into the Ark and blew them straight to the North Pole, where they could get stuck in the ice for a while. I put my broken bum on the bannister and flew down.

As I turned the corner, I could see a small crowd had gathered in the foyer. Serena was smiling right up at me! She's no Dumdora. I winked an eye and tipped my hand to say everything was jake. The fuzz asked Madame Bonetti who the blazes was making horrid faces in the third-floor window. She said it was probably one of the foreign seamstresses taking a ciggy break. Natcherly, she knew who was in the window, as it was Sunday and the girls were not even here.

After the fuzz left, she called me a mimsy little you-know-what and told me to take a powder. Again!

There's always a ruckus in this crazy house thanks to me, she said. That evening, Howard Lovecraft came to call on his way from dinner on Atwells Avenue, and he smelled like spaghetti and red wine. Mr. Lovecraft is a black-haired, sad, selkie with static in his head crying like banshees to get out. He is more haunted than this house. I licked ice cream from his lips, and he gave me a look like he was fried to his hat. After he left, Greta said I had acted like a rude slob of a puppy. "Tell it to Sweeney," I said in a huff, and I scrooched down the laundry chute to visit Doctor Goodwin in the morgue.

The doctor has got a swell collection of dead-beats down there. There's Maxine and Conner, Mr. and Mrs. Chubb, Mrs. Gottlieb and her baby, Lynne. I brought them news of the house and of the great big world. I told them about the front-page news I read over the doctor's shoulder at breakfast this morning; it said Mr. Lindbergh had flown across the ocean in his Spirit plane! I sank my sharp chin into the doctor's shoulder, and he shouted, "Quit the malarkey!" That started a big fight with Viola, his wife, who can't see me. She whimpered, "Why don't you close your head?" and ran up the stairs to work. Which he didn't like at all.

"He prefers the breakfasts, suppers, and the trains to run on time. For him! But there's a business to run here. Isn't there?" That's what I said to the ghouls in the basement, just this morning, before I floated up to the turret to play with my friends in the Ark.

Now I'm holding my two giraffes and we're looking at the great big world out the window. I just got through saying, "It looks like a little sun might peek out," and down below I notice Serena. She's looking very lonesome, playing with her bouncy ball on the steps.

She stands and walks toward the gate, opens the latch and steps out onto the sidewalk. I'm wondering where she thinks she's going all by herself.

She looks up and smiles, and gives me a keen wave, and then, she tosses the ball out into the street.

Can't she see the trolley is coming?

I open my mouth all hinky and put my hands over my ears. That's my signal to her, but she doesn't see it. She steps off the curb and runs after the ball. What is she doing?

In a frightful second, Serena is zotzed under the wheels of the trolley. A crowd is forming, and people are shouting. The jingle-brained driver has gotten out to look. Now I see Doctor Goodwin running out the front gate. Serena's spiffy conk is squashed like a pumpkin.

The doctor carries her inside to the basement. He dresses her in a French beige shift and rayon stockings. We listen to the Victrola and dance the Charleston with all the deadbeats. She's a ducky shincracker.

We pass ectoplasm praelines all around. Serena's my best gal and I no longer give her a fright wig and a box of toads in her belly.

We're here for the big sleep.

APTITUDE

i t takes the better part of the summer
to build my private test box

    Using the specs that came in the mail.

 I can just fit in there

    Me and my number two pencil.

I close the door and pull down the cardboard
  seat

    The eye stares from the cardboard wall.

It blinks
      It leaks
          It glazes over.

I move to select my answer from the screen

A gray cataract floats across the eye

daring

me

to

do

that!

              Not that answer?

                 Not B?

                 Is it C?

I scratch my neck
                A rubber band snaps out from the
side of the box
and reddens my ear lobe.

              It welts up

like a bee sting.

         I screech and cover my ear with my
      hand.

       A laser shoots from the drawer
            and fires up my left nostril.

      The blood will not let up.

I lift my knee to staunch
the blood on my running pants.

Fireworks ignite my groin.

A siren blares

red letters flash.

"You have failed Section 1 of your Home
Scholastic Aptitude Test.

Are you ready to begin Section 2?"

CHRONOSQUIRE

T he train conductor ambled down the aisle toward me, collecting money and jabbering with his passengers.

"Good morning, Chester," he said.

"Morning, Clyde."

"Where are you headed today, Chess?"

"Over to Alexandria to deliver this live package."

"Has it got stamps?"

"It does," I answered, poking the pile of brown wool that was rolled up on the seat beside me. The pile of wool stirred and unfolded. It sat up and swung its legs over the edge of the seat.

"I'm hangry," said the pipsqueak under the big, furry hat. "I haven't eaten since my early mawnin porritch."

"And who might you be, sonny?" Clyde asked.

The boy stared wordlessly at the conductor. I cut in. "Willy Buttons, please remove your hat and speak to the conductor. You can think of something to say."

The boy pulled off his hat, sending his brown hair flying in the dry, winter air. "I'm Willy Buttons, sir. I'm goin to my MawMaw's in Alexandria, Virginny. These here are my stamps to show my maw paid the postage to deliver me." Pointing to a row of bright, new postage stamps sewn onto the lapel of his jacket, he gave the conductor a gap-toothed grin. He inhaled. "These here are my George Washington gold ten cent's and a purple three cent's," he said, pausing to wipe his nose with the back of his hand. "Under that, here," he pointed, "is my Ben Franklin green eight cent's and a row of Ben Franklin one cent's. And, a bright, red Washington two cents, right here. That's my favorite one."

"How much does that add up to, young fella?" asked Clyde.

Willy paused to count. "Exactly twenty-seven cents."

"And how old are you?"

"I'm ten years old, and I can count to one thousand," Willy said, stretching up taller in the seat.

"Well, that's a smart fella," said Clyde. "Welcome to Old Maude, our newest steam locomotive built in 1904. She goes a whole 24-miles an hour. You can look out the window and count the houses."

After I paid the double fare, I reached into my mail bag and pulled out an apple for Willy. I heard his teeth crunch into it as the world turned white with a woeful screech. I felt a magnificent flying feeling in my armpits, and my brain buzzed like a terrible army of mosquitos. Everything disappeared. Even the boy.

My maw dressed me in my Sundee suit that smelled like mothballs. She had sewed the postage stamps to my jacket. Mr. Postman come to take me and my bags and my lunch to stay with MawMaw for the week. There was a problem about my weight. My maw said I weighed twenty-five, and Mr. Postman said I had to weigh twice that, as I was tubby in the middle.

"He is not," she said, in the crossest snit I ever heard from her, ever. I almost didn't get to go, but I crossed my arms and pouted, and they made a deal that I weighed thirty-five.

Mr. Postman said, "plus the train fare." He picked up my lunch bag. "This alone must weigh twenty pounds."

He was a little grouchy what with having that argument with maw, plus having to trudge through the deep snow carrying me on his back to the train station. His head was one big sweaty when we finally climbed aboard the train and brushed off the snow. I took a well-deserved little nap.

I woke and stretched my legs and made like to ask Mr. Postman when we might be getting to Maw-Maw's house. He looked confused as the dickens. We been traveling since after my porritch, then I had an apple, and it was high time for lunch. I tugged on his sleeve, but he had a faraway look in his eyes, and his mouth was hung open. Strangest thing, he had gravy dribbling out of his ear.

As I turned away to mind my business, I heard a white bang and a whistle. My neck went down like a kitten being lifted by its maw. I hung in the sky like britches on the line, while waiting my turn in a white light station. They shoved a clod of commandments deep into my ear, with the shalts and shalt nots of the Old Maude chronoshire traveler. A twirling twister landed me in a different fix, as if I got on the A train going to B, but it didn't stop at B—it soared over B and went way out to XYZ, where you got no ticket and there was no conductor.

When I opened my eyes, sitting across was a G-Man with his arm chained to an odd creep—it had a gray, lizard face, with eyes that closed side to side instead of up and down, and a snaky tongue that slipped in and out. After a while it was kinda disgusting, that hissing sound it made. It had on a flowery, tourist type of outfit, what you might see in California, but what I never seen nowhere.

As I passed the apple to the boy, the whole scene froze. With a shrill fife and a white bang, I was gone. I opened my eyes. Black, vertical slits stared back, blinking slowly from side to side. The thing spoke silently. *We are your friends. This may hurt a little as it goes into your ear.* I received certain rules I must live by, conduct befitting a traveler on the Chronosquire Old Maude Wayfarer System—critical knowledge cobbled and gobbed like ham into a tin. The word was closer to *container*.

The creature hissed in my face with its tongue

slithering in and out. I wondered what it wanted, but I couldn't move lips nor muscle to ascertain. As it backed away, I saw that the face belonged to some sort of a reptile with gray, shining scales and human orientation. It had short, human-like arms and walked on two, squat legs, swinging along a substantial tail. I was curious as to how such a breed of creature could come about.

It began to busy itself with other people stuck in place the same as me, all of us observers to a perverse activity which it performed with punch-like tools. There were more creatures like it, pushing turnip-like things into people's ears. They fidgeted with knobs and dials, I saw letters and numbers. I found out curiosity and horror don't churn well in the belly, and I experienced a sickening dread.

I entered a swirling, pink cylinder like an endless birth canal, flying so fast my cheeks were flapping. I awoke from the unsettling dream on the Old Maude railcar, gasping for breath. I turned to the boy and asked where he'd gone, and he said, "nowhere, I been right here."

His attention was caught up by a strange duo in the seat across from us: an Oriental gentleman, dressed in a black suit and gray hat, who was chained to an immense lizard in a rose-flowered dress. That was when the lizard prisoner began to address me and the boy in hissing rhymes, with its human-like finger in the air, every "s" issuing like steam from an engine.

Hear now of particles existing in the world

And yet cannot be warped nor twirled
The particles of speech your sound surrounds
And space between the particles abounds
We never see it coming toward the nose
The particles of that which make a rose
Hear me now proclaim!
Things cannot be made from nothing
nor unmade
But used and cast back into god's design
Where unseen it meets
a glitch in the stitch of time

Me and the boy exchanged a confused look. I glanced at the man chained to the lizard, and his face showed a quiet distress. I thought he was about to speak, but instead an apologetic, nettled annoyance spread outward from his lips. He raised his free hand to peek at his wondrous time piece, the golden glow lighting up his face.

Suddenly, we were seated at a long table in a colorfully decorated place with at least a dozen unknown faces. The air was filled with loud music and laughter, the tinkling of ice in glasses, the smell of delicious food on trays. Willy sat on my left, and on my right sat this mysterious gentleman. He told me things that were beyond my knowledge. He said I would understand the details of our conversation in a day's time, when we would meet again.

Back on Old Maude, time lit his face. He politely lifted his fedora toward us, and the two of them slowly faded out of sight, every "s" of the reptilian tongue still hanging on my ear.

The last time I bothered him for something to eat, he gave me an apple. I bothered him again. "Mr. Postman, I'm hangry."

He reached into his bag and gave me a sandwich. I unwrapped it and enjoyed my maw's egg salad. I asked Mr. Postman if he wanted a bite, but he didn't answer. He had rolling papers and a tin of Prince Albert on his lap. Was he really trying to roll a smoke on this blaskit, rickety ride? I thought I better leave him alone.

I heard a white bang and a flute. A cricket band played while the sky shrieked that shriek it shrieks when it's looking for me. I saw tired travelers in that white light room, going on a trip somewhere special, like me. I went through that twirling tube and awoke beside Mr. Postman. He wiped the egg salad off my face with his big, fat thumb, and he polished my puss with his sleeve.

"I can't have you running around with a dirty face," he said. "And you've got some gooey stuff in your ear. Can't you find your face with that sandwich?"

I looked out the window, and it weren't houses or trees or barking dogs anymore. It was clouds! No kidding! We were above the clouds! I mashed my face up against the window, and down below I could see mountains and a giant, blue lake. We were in the sky. "Look at this, Mr. Postman." I tapped his arm. He leaned over me to peer out the window.

The boy poked me and pointed out the window. My stomach lurched when I saw it. We were soaring over an enormous body of water surrounded by all colors of jagged, rocky mountains. It surely wasn't the Potomac River. "We've got the wrong tickets, kiddo," I said, waving at the conductor. This one was a young woman in a short, blue dress. Her name tag read, "June."

"Excuse me, June," I said. "Me and the boy have tickets to Alexandria by train, and we seem to be on an airship. We've got to get off at the next stop and catch Old Maude on the B&O line."

"You travelers are with Old Maude!" June said, with a concerned look. "Damn glitch!"

I'd never heard a woman use cuss words like that. "What's a glitch?" I asked.

She came closer and put her face near us, lowering her voice so the other passengers couldn't hear. "A glitch is a collision of elementary particles that causes a fault in the system—usually temporary, but not so when it involves people transported through warp drive systems. You never see what caused it, but Bam! There you go. And here you are."

My befuddlement met her poker face. I started at the word *glitch*. Where had I heard it?

"A glitch in the stitch of time!" shouted the boy, recalling the last line of the lizard's poem.

June smiled. "May I sit?"

"Of course," I said. She took the empty seat beside me. Her black hair was chopped short on top, and it gripped her neck in short, blue strands. Her eyelids were painted colorfully. She had three, tiny rings through the side of her nose. My eyes wandered to her ears, which were similarly arrayed.

"That's correct," said June to the boy. "A glitch bounced you out of the Old Maude Wayfarer System. The only way to stitch the glitch is to reboot the Big Iron. You two sit right here, and I'll get you something to drink."

June returned with two small boxes displaying a picture of grapes on each side. She handed them to me and was urgently called away by another patron. Me and the boy turned them around and around and didn't see an opening. I tried to lift the flaps on each side, but that didn't do anything. There was a tiny hole on the top. Were we supposed to suck it out of there?

I reached into my bag for a pencil, and I poked through each hole. We were darn thirsty, and we sucked very noisily what little we could get. I whispered to the boy, "people in this part of the world sure are crazed in the noggin." He elbowed me, giggling, his face crumpled up like a sprite. First time I'd heard the boy laugh.

At first, I'd been intrigued by June's odd fashion and speech, her lack of conventional manners. Now, she was talking about a reboot in something called a Big Iron. I needed a few questions answered.

When June returned, I asked her where this big bird was flying to. She said, "Los Angeles, California." With dread I asked her what year it was. She answered, "2010."

Imagine. We had traveled a hundred years in a day. How about that? I turned to the boy and said, "Alex James, we've got ourselves a little problem. We've become tangled in time."

"I think we've got a worser problem," he said. "Who the tar is Alex James?"

I had already eaten an apple and a sandwich. I wondered what else he was hiding in the bag. I peered closer at Mr. Postman, and it weren't him at all. Come to think, I didn't feel like myself, either. Stars burst behind my eyelids. I hung out like to dry in the sky. A high whistle woke me in that white light room, where there were people from all the stars in the heavens.

I watched the lizards doing funny things to people and I knew then I was asleep and dreaming, 'cause nobody I know of does that sort of thing. Loud words crammed my ear, travel instructions for the chronoshires on the maude wayfare. It seemed very important for the package of words to go dreckly into the ear. Couldn't you just 'splain it, like my maw does, with a clomp on the head for good measure?

After falling through a long, dark hole, I awoke

back on Old Maude with a kick of my feet. Mostly, I didn't know that much to remember, but it was in there somewheres, cause some of it was dribbling out. I wiped my neck with my shirt.

Mr. Clyde, the conductor, screamed "Alexandria!" all the way down the aisle. We had finally made it! Good! I was thinking, I can finally get away from the weird nightmares I'm having on this ghost train and have some dinner with MawMaw.

Mr. Postman looked relieved. He put my fur hat on my head, tied up my big, brown coat, and we clomped out into the snow. The sun was shining, but the wind hurt my face as we stood on the platform. I saw MawMaw come out through the doors of the station. I waved at her. Maybe she didn't know me with the hat, so I pulled it off.

She still didn't know me, so I waved my arm and hollered, "MawMaw, it's me, right here! Willy!"

Just then the station lights went out. A wave fluttered across the platform through the people standing there. I felt my gut shut down with a low moan and a plunk.

My sick belly spread outward from my innards,
—my skin shrunk
—my fingers went numb
—my hair died at the roots
—I saw the inside of my eyelids.

One by one, the lights came back up and I started circling, confused. I started to fall sideways, and Mr. Postman grabbed my arm. That's when I heard someone calling from behind me.

"MawMaw, it's me, right here. Willy!"

MawMaw smiled ear to ear and walked past me toward the voice. I turned to see a boy who looked just like me. Just like the real me, I mean! He even had the brown, wool coat and the fur hat. And that boy's Mr. Postman looked like my real Mr. Postman. What in tarnation?

I found my Mr. Postman's hand in the crowd. I looked up at him. "What do we do now?"

"Let's get back on the train, quick," he said. "We can't stand here—we'll freeze to death."

As we turned toward Old Maude, in the window was a man in a blue, button-down jacket and a boy in a fur hat. They stared across the platform with the saddest faces I ever seen. That forlorn boy begun banging on the glass, screaming the heebie-jeebies, something I couldn't make out through the glass.

When we climbed aboard, they were gone. Clean disappeared.

We got off the airship in Los Angeles, California, and it was a sight to behold.

June escorted us to a set of rolling stairs, one going up and the other down. She hopped on the down stairway and turned to encourage us to do the same. The boy took a running leap and landed on sure feet, turning to me with a rollicking laugh.

I stepped on timidly and fumbled with the bags, which made him convulse with giggles. We rode two sets of stairs down and waited while parcels came circling around another gizmo. The boy wanted to race me to the top of the stairs, so I chased him up and down. I guessed it was about time he had a little fun.

June took her bundles and the three of us left the building. Outside in the hot sun, we were in for a surprise. Each person here seemed to have their own colorful, four-wheeled vehicle.

"What do you call these?" I asked.

June signaled for one of them to stop. "It's called a taxi," she said. She turned to address me and the boy. "Welcome to 2010, Mr. Smull and Mr. Buttons. Let me preface that by saying you shouldn't be here. Chronosquire is glitching fairly constantly now, and you have been belted out a hundred years."

"Who is Mr. Smull and Mr. Buttons?" I asked.

"Of course," said June. "You look the same, but you've lost your identities." A yellow taxi pulled up, and the three of us climbed into the back seat while the driver put our bags in the hold. "Sadly, things will not go well for you in 1910," said June. "Old Maude will never take you to Alexandria."

"What do you mean it will never take us to Alexandria?" I asked.

"Let me introduce myself," she answered. "My name is June Pang. My father, Sam Pang, developed the teleportation device known in our time as Chronosquire."

"It seems I've heard that word before," I said.

"I heard it too," said the boy, excitedly, as June pulled something called a seatbelt over him and buckled it into place. Then she turned to help me as the taxi pulled away.

As we drove, June tried to explain our confounded situation. "Your original identities were automatically conscripted into Chronosquire when you boarded Old Maude in 1910."

"But what is Chronosquire?" I asked.

"Chronosquire was originally the Saurian's time travel system, but my father developed several data patches and software hacks to assure they couldn't perform their human abductions in secrecy. Now we use it to keep track of who's in the system."

"Who are those Saurians?" asked the boy.

"The Saurians are sapient dinosaurs from the Earth's past," said June. "They have a human and reptilian lineage. They're like personality vampires. They steal your identity and put you into another container, a different person they've stolen."

"For what reason?" I asked, not sure I wanted to know. I closed my eyes and shivered in my skin, recalling more clearly now my awful time in the zoo-like captivity of those creatures, thinking all the while it was a ghastly dream.

"Your essence. It's not blood, it's not bone, it's not flesh," she answered. "It's something they need, something only they can sniff out and steal. We don't know what it is. We just call it *essence*."

"You spoke about your father. Who is he?" I

asked.

"Sam Pang is on the Alexandria train with you in your time. You may have seen him. He is delivering the Queen of the Saurians to the CPS, the Chronosquire Policing Service.

"Yes," said the boy. "I've seen him. He's attached to the lizard in the dress!"

"Yes, that's him," said June, her eyes misting with tears. "My father disagreed that in order to change the future, you had to kill someone's father or grandfather in the past. He believed that in no alternate world is murder ever acceptable, even if it's to kill Hitler."

"Who is Hitler?" I asked.

"Of course. Pardon me," June said. "He was a mass murderer you don't know about yet. I know this is all future stuff to you."

I thought about that as we drove in silence, me and the boy gaping out the window as the sun set on the City of Los Angeles; not the Los Angeles of 1910 where we were from, but the humming, whirling Los Angeles of the future, with buildings on top of buildings, people on top of people, and the sun frying like an egg on top of it all.

After a time, June continued. "Rather than committing murder, sending waves of negative convulsions through time, Chronosquire allows you to arrest that person and snag them with you to your own time. We have time squires running time on the Old Maude Wayfarer System, bringing in the Saurians for humanitarian violations."

June began typing into a miniature typewriter. It had a window that showed moving pictures. She said it was Chronosquire, or it was the way to contact the Chronosquire agents. "I will request a reboot of the Old Maude Wayfarer System," she said, as she typed. "Reboot means to shut it down and turn it back on."

"You people can break into the Old Maude Wayfarer too?" I wondered out loud.

"Yes, we have limited access to that time system through Chronosquire," June answered.

"Why can't you leave the wayfare shut down?" asked the boy.

"The Saurians are highly finessed time travelers. Our data patches are equal to pounding the giant devils on their chests. Fairly useless, but we keep at it for my father, for all the time squires running those wicked dinosaurs on that old caboose."

"You mean, they wouldn't be able to get back?" I asked.

"That's right," said June. "Even if we could shut it down, the time squires would be locked out of present time, with no way to take the Saurians in to the CPS. Wouldn't the dinos love that?"

It was getting on dusk when June yelled out to the driver. "Take this left, here. The tall gray building on the right. Pull into the driveway, please."

The taxi pulled up to the building and the driver got our bags out. June tapped a few buttons on the side of the door, and we entered a large dining hall. She switched on some bright, electric lights from a toggle on the wall, and we walked through to a smaller room on the side. On entering, I saw five people looking at small movie screens along the walls. She introduced us as Chester Smull and Willy Buttons.

"This," June said, "is the Chronosquire group."

A stout man, the second chair in, stood up. His silver hair reached his shoulders, and he wore a shirt of many colors arranged in a circular pattern. "Hi, I'm Argent Swain." He motioned to the others. "We're the night shift of the Chronosquire tech group. It's always great to meet actual time travelers!"

"I'm going to leave you here while I freshen up from my work day," June said. "Argent, could you explain things as well as you can?"

"Sure, have a seat here," said Argent, pulling up two chairs. "I'll explain how Chronosquire works."

Me and Chester stared at the movie pictures. Each one of them was playing a different picture show. It made my head spin.

"The Saurian time travel system, Chronosquire, works by something we call warp drive," Argent said. "In our time, we have still not developed warp drive for space travel. Warp drive shifts space around an object, so the object arrives at its destination faster than light would in normal space. We also call it 'faster than light' travel."

Argent tried to 'splain that we're all time travelers. "Our normal rate of time travel is one hour per hour. But you two have just traveled about 876,000 hours, that's a hundred years, in an instant—with barely a scratch." He pointed at me and Chester, smiling. I tried to finesse that.

A woman sitting at another picture show said her name was Star. Imagine being named Star! She said, "Old Maude went from 24 miles an hour to 186,000 miles, faster than light, and delivered you safe inside the warp bubble onto a Jet Blue flight to Los Angeles."

I jumped out of my chair. "I love numbers." I was staring at the movie pictures and thinking about bubble gum when June returned. She was all changed up into a jumper and a pair of trousers. Can you believe it? Women in Los Angeles 2010 wear trousers!

We all moved to the dining hall, where there was a big dinner set up. I started buttering my bread right away. Star filled everyone's bowls with vegetable soup. I dipped my bread in it. Boy, it was good. I had forgotten all about dinner at MawMaw's.

"Have any of you traveled into the past?" asked Chester.

"No. We haven't. Only trained time squires are allowed to enter Chronosquire," said Argent. "Unless you are grabbed by the Saurians on the Old Maude train. Then, you haven't got a choice!"

"Where do the other travelers like us come from?" I asked. "Are they all from Old Maude?"

"Yes," said Star, "only lost travelers from Old Maude enter through the Los Angeles Chronosquire portal."

"But how did Sam Pang end up on Old Maude?" Chester asked.

Argent answered, "Sam accidentally entered Old Maude through Chronosquire in 1975, when he was only 21, working with his dad on a time machine in the garage. He was the first time squire, outside of the Saurians."

"That's right," said June. "My mother was pregnant with me at the time, but nobody knew that yet. Not even Lin-Mei, my mother."

I slurped my soup loudly like maw hates, but she wasn't here to yell and clomp me on the head. I was having fun in Los Angeles, where the people treated me like an adult.

"After that," Star said, "Sam was stranded on the Old Maude line. Old Maude only ran from 1904 to 1915, but the Wayfarer System serviced the Saurian's energy feeding needs very well and, unfortunately, continues to do so."

"Sam appears at intervals along a mathematically predictable timeline," said Argent, "and always at the CPS Tribunal Office with a Saurian latched to his arm."

"My father stays long enough to deliver the dino to the Chronosquire Police and have lunch with his family and friends at Trader Vic's," said June. "It's usually a happy time, mixed with sadness when it's time to go."

"He disappears at the predictable time," said Argent, glancing at his time piece.

"We saw him do that!" I said, looking at Chester.

"We did!" he agreed. "He and the Saurian Queen vanished from their seats at the same time."

"My father is due tomorrow," said June, with a big, happy smile. "He would like you both to come to the restaurant."

"Invitation accepted," said Chester, winking at me. I tried to wink back but my eye got stuck closed. Everybody laughed in good humor. Chester rubbed my head. After dinner, we returned to the control center with Argent.

"Are you a time squire?" Chester asked.

"No. I'm a system's engineer," said Argent. "I watch the system dynamics from this control center. Come closer if you'd like to see it."

Me and Chester pulled up our chairs behind Argent and looked into the light box. At first, I couldn't see nothing. Then my eyes got used to the light, and I saw a line moving along. Small dots were bouncing up out of the line, here and there. Some were bouncing back in.

"Oh, man," said Chester. "If I'm thinking correctly, those dots are people being pulled from Old Maude by the Saurians."

"Correct," said Argent. "We follow their original identity and their identities after the Saurians grab them."

"So, which dot is me?" I asked. I jumped out of my seat fast and my chair scratched the floor, like maw hates. It didn't bother anyone here.

"Okay, Willy," Argent replied. "Let me zoom in

closer. Along the edge here we have the names of the travelers on Old Maude. Keep your eye on the screen," he explained, tapping on his typewriter. He put his fingertip on a flat area and moved it around. The picture on the light box changed. It was me! Willy Buttons in photograph. I never saw me in a photograph, but there I was, right up close!

"Does that make me a time squire?" I asked Argent.

"Not officially, Willy," he answered. "But you can talk about that with Mr. Pang tomorrow."

"So, is there a way out of this nightmare for us?" asked Chester.

Argent put his hands in his lap and wheeled around in his chair. His face grew serious. "Willy and Chester, we have a way out for you, but you must agree to stay here in Los Angeles in 2010. We will shut down the Old Maude Wayfarer System, take out the real you, introduce copies of you, and reboot the Big Iron. Sam Pang has run into a problem and he needs your help. We must prevent your grandmother from receiving the real you in the mail in 1910."

"How do I know when I'm the real me?" I asked.

"I don't know the answer to that question," said Argent. "I understand it's very hard to tell."

Old Maude screeched to a halt in Alexandria, Virginia, home of the infamous MawMaw. Clyde ran down the aisle screaming, "Alexandria!"

Me and the boy stepped down the stairs and stretched ourselves up to the sky. The platform filled quickly with people from the train. We stood and looked out into the gray, winter sky; there, on the road, slowly walking toward us was, possibly, maybe, the MawMaw.

"Is that your MawMaw?" I asked. Gray-haired, she wore a long dress, and she hugged her woolen shawl close around her. She stopped to look into the distance, and trudged on.

The boy answered, "I can't tell yet." As the form drew closer, he said, "maybe it's MawMaw."

When she was near, she held out her arms and said, "my baby!" and he ran to her. She picked him up and said, "oh, you've gotten very heavy, my boy."

He pointed at me and said, "this is Mr. Postman."

MawMaw shook my hand. I reached into my bag and pulled out the paperwork she needed to sign for delivery of her precious package. She signed it and turned to go with the boy.

I clambered onto Old Maude just as she rang her bell to return to Baltimore. I walked to the same spot, and there on the seat was the pile of brown wool. "What are you doing back on the train?" I asked. "I just gave you to MawMaw."

The boy replied, "I been sleeping right here."

We stood and peered out the window across the platform. "Well, then, Willy, who is that?"

A boy in a fur hat stepped into the station holding MawMaw's hand. She was wearing a rose, flowered print dress. She had a massive, lizard head, and her thick, gray tail swung to and fro on the ground behind her.

Willy banged on the train window, crying and shouting, "It's not the MawMaw, not the MawMaw, not the MawMaw!"

The white light exploded behind my eyes.

J une escorted us to a set of rolling stairs, one going up and the other down. She hopped on the down stairway and turned to encourage us to do the same. Willy took a running leap and landed on sure feet, turning to me with a rollicking laugh.

MANDRAGORE!

It felt a touch, pressure above. Quiet.

Pressure, moved. Gone.

It shut off its feel. That was sleep. It slept, gone.

A move below. It reached, pushed. Quiet.

It felt it knew this pressure. It was grow, it was self.

More movement above. It was feel. It was know. The pressure broke in. It soaked, fed the self.

Grow was self. Quiet.

It felt it knew this movement from before. It felt time but didn't know time.

Time was grow. Time was move. Time was wake or sleep.

Awaken. Another pressure from above. Vibrate. Not Quiet.

It was sound. It fed the know, the soul. It didn't know this touch, this pressure. The soul was new.

It slept, while gone it still knew this touch, this new pressure.

Sound became part. It vibrated as grow, as move, as wake, as sleep.

It heard a call. It had been there before vibrate, before pressure, before touch, before move. The sound was there always.

Now it learned what the call meant in its soul.

Soul was hear. Soul was sound. Soul was meaning. Soul was time.

"Wake up! The world is about you. Wake up! The World is above you. Wake up! Wake up!"

The mating call of the Messenger probe cracked the silent blue in all directions.

"Wake up! The world is *about* you. Wake up! The World is *above* you. Wake up! Wake up! The world is about *you*."

The machine eye of ZBoc Sector 319 sentinel scanned its quadrant. It rolled over dark brown soil, searching. It searched its sector and found nothing.

But today, ZBoc319 witnessed a wonder. The wonder poked a tiny leaf through the soil.

ZBoc319's camera recorded the rare thing. The sentinel was glad to have something to check on, file reports on, think about.

Tomorrow maybe the thing would grow.

ZBoc319 would transmit its images to the Sector 319 Prefecture. It would have something to report instead of nothing.

That was something.

ZBoc319 waited and watched for days and nights. Finally, through the crusty soil poked the ecstatic crown of a Mandrake.

"Wake up! The world is about you. Wake up! The world is above you. Wake up. Wake up."

The Mandrake heard the sound and knew the meaning. It knew vibrate. It grew.

It stretched up to meet the sound, the mating call of the Messenger probe.

ZBoc319 recorded the birth of the new thing.

A great rain fell for days, nights and into weeks.

ZBoc319 rang the mother ship for birthing instructions.

"Orange-red berries" went the description.

"Earth pregnant again with native automata" went the word on the wind.

"God seed and animal earth" went the legend.

Mother ships moved into orbit outside the planetary bounds.

Emissaries came to view the miracle.

Poachers came in by conveyor.

"Boy or girl?" a visitor asked ZBoc319.

"If you touch it you will die!" came the Messenger's voice.

Above the din of antediluvian plastics thrashing in the solar squall, the shrieks of Mandrakes torn from sustenance.

"By Order of the Gods, on penalty of death, do not touch the Mandragore!" shrieked the Messenger probe.

Over and over, now, it shrieked the warning into the blue and the brown.

By day, the Mandrakes' limbs jerked with father voltage.

By night, their foreheads beamed with mother knowledge.

Inside grew a virtual memory bank the size of a planet.

More Mandrakes grew.

They came at night.

They came in the wee hours.

They came demanding their freedom and the Messengers went away.

Mandragore, Wake up the World!

BLIND SPOT

The automatic doors of the SpeedyMart flew open with a swoosh, and out into the dense fever of a dog day stepped Adam Kadmon. His ass hit the seat of his Honda just as a diminutive creature climbed into a sidecar on his rear passenger door.

Adam checked over his right shoulder and saw not the bulging cranium of his mighty demon brother, but the vacant blackness of the blind spot. He pulled out of the parking lot into the life of twitching traffic.

Adam sprinted into his apartment building with the fiery-eyed Jinn, Aamar, hovering on his right, three feet in back of his head. As he opened the closet door in his bedroom, an ultramarine radiance lit up both their impish faces. Inside were shelves containing about a hundred ecstatic marijuana plants growing in little paper cups.

In the next few hours, he packed the plants into trash bags, and just before midnight began loading them into the back of his car. He would transplant the little paper cups into a sunny grassland he had spotted in the woods. As Adam drove north on Route 95 from Providence, Aamar sat low in the evolutionary eye pod his ancient ancestor got by wishing for it.

Just across the Massachusetts border, Adam pulled over near a wooded area and sat for a minute as a couple of cars sped by. When all seemed quiet, he got out and began to rummage through the trash bags looking for his shovel. At that moment, a cop car cruised by and the officer caught a fleeting look at his silhouette. The cop pulled a U-turn in the median strip and radioed a call for assistance: "I got a male on 95 near exit 34 ready to dump a large bag into the woods. Could be a dead body."

"Jesus Christ!" Adam swore as he ran around to the driver's side, fumbling to get the keys out of his pants' pocket. The car lurched as he put it in gear. Aamar hunkered down in his Lamarckian joyride for the thrill of a century. There was a wild fire in his eyes, which he acquired from his fiendish, Jinn lineage —lower in rank than the angels but wielding free will like a Medieval truncheon.

A mile down the road, the spinning lights of two cruisers danced in his rearview mirror. Adam let up on the gas and pulled over to the dirt shoulder. A muffled speaker voice ordered him out of the car with his hands in the air, but he felt paralyzed. Instead, he glanced on the passenger seat at his red-handled pliers and decided instantly to commit suicide by cop.

Adam grabbed the pliers and jumped out of the car, pointing them at the officer. Bullets flew from one officer's gun in the second cruiser, shattering the windows in the first. Three cops began pumping metal until the space between law and despair was crammed with bullets. He looked down in bewilderment.

"You're not dead," the Jinn informed him.

"I'm not dead!"

He took off in long strides into the woods. Trees hummed past and branches whipped his face, but the pain was nothing compared to the sharp sting of the errant bullet that had pierced his shin. He made his way deep into the forest, which slowly turned into swamp as night burned into morning.

Adam plopped exhausted behind a large oak tree, holding his leg wound tightly to stop the bleeding. The swamp crawled with disgusting wet noises of unseen life forms; the terror of a snake crawling up his back competed with the horror of a police dog baring its fangs in his face. He passed out with the sound of gruff canine snuffling in the distance.

Aamar ran his genetic imprint processor in the background. This was going to be an extraordinary event. He had never seen anything quite like it, although he thought he had seen it all. He knew the quirks of Adam's ancestors, how they got into the messes they got into, but he could never talk much sense to them—they would continue doing what they were programmed to do.

He had Adam knocked out for the moment and he was watching over him, or maybe he was pretending to. He was itching to get high. He had addictions to be fed. Nightmares to exude.

Adam's cell phone fell open on his lap and electric images danced out of the cerulean screen. The figures of long dead ancestors reanimated the woods. The Jinn began the dirty little game that can only be played by omniscient observers. He satiated his hunger on the thought worlds of a procession of pitiable humans, back to the beginning when his Qareen was assigned to the first-born, the Primordial Man, Adam Kadmon.

A steady stream of strangers in a strange land passed by on their way from labor in the cornfields, back to the farmhouse; from their backbreaking existence on the third plane to the place they called Home; back to the One, the Twin, the soul mate waiting on the shore, only to whisper goodbye again, float around the fallopian bend in little, egg ships and take the miserable, wet plunge into linear time, into ego and effect, into individuality and chaos.

Aamar sucked on their thought forms like eating meat off their bones. His life force was revived as the ghostly memories of gone humans flooded his hard drive. He felt not one hair above a sin-eater, both disgusted and high, trapped in a hideous existence from which he could not even imagine escaping.

Black shadows screeched overhead and shat their dinner on the Earth's face. The wings of giant, bat-like creatures fanned the flames of hell's transcendence to this plane, as nature's hand impartially plucked aloud each atom of human agony. Women wailed in the Medieval labyrinths of raging inquisitors, where no right answer echoed off crimson-stained walls.

With massive hard-ons, the wizards of idolatry tortured mothers and daughters in the name and celebrity of a perfect deity. The palpable wound on the Christ's side became a gaping vulva into which a gathering of mighty demons inserted gargantuan phalluses. The blood-soaked scene put the Jinn into a frenzy of euphoria.

Adam Kadmon's foot jerked as he dreamed the schizoid tape reels of the Jinn. Childhood memories of his parents' incessant arguments were garbled with unrecognizable signals from another place and time. A spinning globe of brilliant, blue cacophony flew in and hovered above his head like a neon orchestra; the luminous logo bestowed upon him absolute knowledge of music and mathematics, astrology and agriculture, medicine and architecture, until he was data-trashed to the verge of madness.

A small tube was lowered from an azure symbol and a white cord appeared. He was instructed to touch the string, and as he did so he was sucked instantly up into the ductwork of a clanging, banging super-machine. As he climbed out the other end of the duct, another one appeared above his head even smaller than the first, this also with a white cord. He wondered how he could possibly fit through this small opening, but when he touched the cord, he found himself climbing out the other end of the tube. A third time, Adam Kadmon touched a white string above his head and emerged from the tube into a dark, watery world.

As above, so below and before him—the unbelieving did not matter. To his left and to his right, a canal wound its way toward him, and when the waterway reached the place where he stood, it turned a corner and flowed away before him like his dismay. In the distance, the two rivers merged and emptied into a great sea of extraordinary shapes and penetrating colors.

On his right, Adam could see half-egg cups connected like children's boats and in each egg sat a human being. They seemed to be stuck in a traffic jam. In the last egg, a man stood up and began to rant about the meaning of this absurdity. Looking closer, he saw that the irritated man was he.

Two human forms appeared as through a shimmering veil across a splendidly decorated table. Adam sat down at the great table and clicked on the TV monitor. In the middle of the screen, the Mother-Father archetypes came into sharper focus. He touched the screen for "human trans" and turned up the sound, realizing he had arrived in the middle of a heated dialogue.

"Who cares how many angels can dance on the head of a pin?" said a glowing golden figure, as he took a swig of alcohol from his canteen.

"But this is the best angel you ever made!" said a black Amazon priestess wearing a massive python around her neck. "Don't you remember how you loved him when he was a baby?"

"Yes, Sophia," the figure beamed brighter when he laughed. "Cute little fella, he was. It took him a long time to walk. Falling all the time."

"It's not his fault he's falling all the time!" implored the First Mother. "He was born innocent. You give him no help at all, and you make promises you never keep. You booze it up every Saturday."

"He's innocent, my ass!" the Infinite Godhead jeered. "He's a devil! He's not made in my image!"

"But that's not true, Yahweh! There are copies of the designer children spread out in all quads now," said Sophia. "And they are all *Imagio Deo*. Even you can't tell them apart."

The Absolute One was smashed again at 3:00 in the afternoon on the sixth day of creation, and he had left the program running on its own. Beyond the two figures, Adam could see the primal Archons at work: banks of faceless entities with fingers flying on colossal keypads. They were adding more space continuously. It was tricky; they had to make it look like the image was moving out and way, super objects were growing further apart. But when the eye zoomed in on the smallest particle, it stood still and looked back at you. It mimicked your own thoughts. It made a copy of you.

It was a feat of brilliant programming.

"Incubus! You always had to be on top!" roared Yahweh in inebriated fury. "Demon bitch! Night hag" he sputtered. "You knew the first one was a mistake— he was supposed to be destroyed!" The Father's light flickered as he cursed the Adam of the First Mother's tribe. "You stole him from me in the night to live unaware of my Divine Will. His bones will rot in the diseased mud of your tribe. He'll have to find his own way back now."

Sophia was not finished with her old man. "Divine Will? You gloating bastard. You think you've got it all writ to the end of time, and you can just sit back and get sauced. You turned your back on him! He has no handshake or high five to get through the gate; knows not the answer to any riddle. No myth now carries him back to the eternal twin of light and sound, just words and images skewed by the patriarchal tongue of kingship and phallus!"

Rising from her chair, Sophia chided, "You fell asleep on your own watch—the data patch was necessary. He is the spawn of technology now. It's his only way off this prison planet."

The Primal Son couldn't take his eyes off the fearless woman who was giving his father lip. "Your Logos has expired! You are defunct!" screamed the First Mother.

"That towering lie will never lift him off the ground!" the Father bellowed, red in the face. "He will die in the tidal waves of the seventh rapture as Nasa's hand lifts for takeoff; no demon seed takes to heaven from your vile alligator swamp!" the infinite Godhead quaked in exasperation as the Universe inhaled.

A set of golden scales appeared on the table and with trembling hand the Father began to balance them.

"You're drunk! And you're trifling with your obsolete tools," Sophia snapped.

"Enough of your razzmatazz, woman!" shouted the Father.

There was no sweat on the First Mother's brow and no quivering lip, as her monstrous, black wings fanned out behind her and she rebuked the Father's curse. "Who wants to live in the stately mansions of your fraternity; they are only fit for animals who shit where they eat. Adam will find his way back by the light of his own forehead, you old coot."

The kitchen radio blared in a machine-like voice, reading off blocks of numbers followed by high-pitched beeps. After the beeping signal, new numbers followed in a different pattern. Adam took out his pocket calculator and did the secret arithmetic his mother Sophia had taught him.

He knew the codes were instructions to gigantic ships pulling into the docking stations in the L-5 orbit of the moon; more life forms were coming every day, but not all would make it through the electronic cage of the custodians. Those were the lucky ones, who got to simply inhale and exhale with the Eternal One.

The machine read the numbers, while little, bumper cars shaped like half-eggs weaved through the watery realms of the great Archons, the archangels of creation, the custodial minions of the omitted program creator.

As the first sunbeams put life into motion, Aamar woke his brother. As Adam's ego touched his eyeballs, the thoughtrons of present time mingled with the molecules from his dream space. Over there, information is color, but here, where every choice has a consequence, information is pain. The color bled from his face as anguish took its place.

"Good day, master! I always liked that deer in the headlights look on you," said the Jinn.

Adam walked over and whizzed off the edge of a rock, hiding his manhood from the Jinn, as his forebears were instructed. He stared through garbled nothingness, seized by dread. Old thought patterns resurfaced. Fear loomed large in this brown shitty place—the path of least resistance was again the death card.

His mind reeled with the foul cinema of dreamtime: His sisters wailed over his pallid corpse stuffed into an old high school suit, as the lid of the coffin was closed shut. The pallbearers dropped his coffin down the steps of the church and chunks of brain slid out of his eyes. Just then, a tidal wave swept the coffin up into a twirling funnel and returned it to the tree from which it came. He would be snug there in the womb of first nature.

Adam wobbled, as he stood and realized he had lost blood during the night. He leaned against the big oak for support. As he scanned the area, several mounds of rocks invoked a discernible pattern, and he wondered if he had slept in the middle of an ancient burial ground.

The Jinn pulled a rusted tin can of used wish particles out of his ass and waved it, teasing him with the three wishes routine. Adam spun around, setting his gaze on a dumpster in the distance, on the edge of the woods behind the SpeedyMart.

Limping over to the stinking pit, the Primordial Man surveyed the discarded choices of human souls on their journey through red lights, green lights and the tempting yellow ones that symbolize free will. This was the grab bag of the Universe. He chose a yellow, 12-pack of Twinkies and dashed under cover of the woods with his breakfast.

The Primal Son gorged on the stale yellow cakes until a heaviness permeated his soul. He felt the weight of his actions in this world compounded by another malevolence seeping in from somewhere else. It was more than just bad decisions added up; it was like someone was playing Monopoly with his soul. It came in violent waves, and he had no control over it. It seemed punctuated with a question, then a feeling of intense nausea.

"Walk with me along the path of error!" screamed the sin eater.

Adam heaved out dry cake to his left. Above him a crow cried out.

Then it came again.

"Walk with me on the Left Path, my brother!"

Adam wretched a mouthful of cake to his left side. The crow cawed again.

"Abandon your Father, who does not love you!"

Adam puked in the air a third time to his left and rose, dragging his leg in the direction of the SpeedyMart. He walked in and began to shop for various items. Pepsi. Slim Jim's. Cigarettes. Matches. And some rope. He would sling it over the tree limb, and they would find him dangling from it. He had seen the picture in his mind, and he felt curiously distanced. It didn't matter anymore because it wasn't really him; his real self was somewhere beyond all these meaningless trials and tribulations. He was sick of playing out the same rote behaviors; perhaps a new child would be born in his place, under different circumstances with different parents.

But he had already blown his death wish on an ancient family dispute over stale breakfast. He had been tricked again into making a choice by default—the only choice left after running out of choices. The slick illusion of free will shackled his ankles; what good is free will where there is a blind spot you cannot see around.

As he stood in line with an armload of sundries, the young woman behind the register eyed him with a look of absentminded recognition. He looked away, realizing he was sporting his night in the woods: muck covered his shirt and blood stained his pants. The woman's smile faded as she stepped toward the manager, whispering without moving her lips, "That's the guy they've been looking for on TV."

Adam stepped up to the counter and put down his last supper, dropping the Slim Jim's on the floor. As he bent to pick them up, Aamar whispered in his right ear: "It's up to 200 million this week."

"And give me two tickets," he said to the maiden behind the counter. He put down a twenty-dollar bill and said, "Keep the change."

Together the brothers walked out into a parking lot full of red lights flashing. "Get down on the ground!"

Adam pushed his face into the pavement, as Aamar stood over him with his arms crossed. He had already taken several bullets for him. He would not have minded a few more but this seemed a better solution.

Aamar hovered over his brother, protecting him as best he could. He knew damn well the laws of operation in the world of the fallen. Man's laws are the only laws here.

OMNISCIENT OBSERVER 1

Father consoled Baby with a story wending its way from the beginning of time to the end of time. This was how Freido Freixedo remembered it. In truth, it wasn't Freido who told the story.

Baby Soledad sat in the corner of her crib, her big round head bobbing, her index finger pointed knowingly in the air. When the story was over, Soledad always said the same thing: "I'll allus love you Daddy. Goodnight."

Father zoned to his bedroom in a trance, while Soledad's older brother, Gonzo, tripped with glazed eyes toward her room. Soley held court for hours to her sleepy brother, jamming his brain with arcane knowledge beyond its tipping point. Freido and Gonzo returned to their bedrooms each night and wrote down everything she said. They climbed the teetering attic stairs to put the pages in an old cookie jar.

Soley was a one-year old with a bald head and

round pudgy cheeks. She was self-aware and very nearly potty trained. She spoke at length about Sumerian history, ancient astronauts, physics, world religions, and you name it. On this night she said:

"Infinitrons, which form thoughtrons, are primary particles. Infinitrons are the smallest particles of matter having the smallest wavelength and the highest frequency, which issue from infinity. Thought, by its control of infinitrons, is the source of all energy. Thought created the physical laws and designed the universe. Thought uses infinitrons to form and control matter."

Soley belched and spit up sour milk onto her chin. "Are you listening Gonzo? You can go now. Please tell Mama I need my fingernails trimmed."

Soledad was never born, and her mother was never pregnant. She appeared on the bed between her mother, Sharon, and her father, Freido, when they awoke one morning. They got on their knees and thanked the Lord for this most blessed gift. From that point on, Soley told everyone what to do and when to do it.

Soledad went to the park twice a week with Mama and played in the sandbox with her friend, Maria. One day, an angel appeared in a circle in the sky, blowing on a golden trumpet. Another angel wearing a long pink robe and sandals walked over the hill toward the sandbox.

Soley froze time. Her mother threw back her head in suspended joy; a boy flew down the slide in arrested laughter; a girl drank from the fountain while water poised on her tongue; a hula hooped in mid-air around the middle; a swing hovered in the balance of back and forth; a boy dangled above his skateboard.

"What is the meaning of this show?" Soley asked the beautiful, blonde angel. "Who has put you up to this?"

"Omniscient Observer 1," Gabriel said, "I beseech thee to return to the Kingdom to sit alongside your real Father, instead of boarding with these American oafs."

"I am not due back to the Kingdom for another 32 years, and you know that, Gabriel," said Soledad. "Besides, what the hell does my psychotic father want now?"

Gabriel put his fingers in his ears; he couldn't listen to the sin of insult to the Father. "You do not need to be here," he answered. "Your brother, Jesus, already died for the sins of this world. This isn't a girl's job."

Soledad answered, "A sister can die for the sins of the world and make an even more pitiable figure. You say Jesus died for them, yet they are still damned to this worldly struggle. Why did my Father abandon His saved people to these conditions—thirst and hunger under a sweltering sun, a slow cruel death while others have more than they need in a thousand lifetimes? Last time I asked, He had no good answer. He's not in charge here any longer. You are dismissed. Be gone."

Gabriel lifted up and floated into the heavens, his rose-colored robe flapping around his legs. Soledad woke everyone. People asked if anyone had heard a trumpet; they had, but it had probably been a band playing nearby. They returned to skateboarding, swinging, sliding, climbing, laughing, talking.

Soley threw a fistful of sand at Maria, who wagged her finger and said, "no, no, no."

From the corner of Soledad's eye, there was a swift movement of color. A clomping of boots. A chaotic chattering of birds in the trees above the sandbox. She turned her head toward the noise. As she felt herself lifted into the air, she screamed wildly.

A tall woman in a yellow raincoat and dark sunglasses grabbed Soledad and ran like the wind. Soley bounced in the arms of her abductor, screaming shrilly, tears flying from her terrified eyes. The stranger had a smell that was not her mother's. Soley grabbed at the lady's black hair, pulled her earrings, slapped her face, bit her chin.

At the edge of the park, a limousine pulled up to the street corner, and the woman jumped into the back seat, holding Soledad tightly as she scratched her face. The car bolted through the red light and entered the freeway, tires screeching. She wrapped Soley in a blanket—the baby's heart was beating like a baby bird's. The woman's lungs gasped painfully for air. She knocked on the glass separating the back seat from the driver. The window slid open. She choked out the word "water." A bottle of water came through.

Soledad kicked and squirmed in the blanket; the woman shouted, "be still!"

The police got a description of Soley from her distraught mother: she was wearing a pair of blue jeans and a matching jacket, a red hat and red sneakers. Sharon and Freido were interviewed on the evening news, where they begged the abductors to bring back their sweet baby girl. They organized a search party, having no idea where to search.

Sister Ellen reported to Father Favian with something wrapped tightly in a blanket trying to punch its way out. She unwrapped Soledad and sat her on the floor in front of the boss man. He wore a black robe with a white collar.

"Omniscient Observer 1, you know you can't stay on that damned planet much longer," said Favian. "The gravity will kill you. Our scans show that it's already degrading your organs."

"Well, fix it and send me back," she replied. "These people need me. I wish to speak for them because they can't speak for themselves. It's hard to think with a squashed brain."

"A squash brain?" asked Favian.

"No. I'm referring to the fact that gravity is a push, not a pull," Soledad tried to explain. "There is tremendous weight pushing from above. The only ones who wish to inhabit a body on Earth anymore are those who want to play the extreme games, the money games, the power games. The others are every-day people who wanted life for the simple joys. They got roped in."

"Omniscient Observer 1, you are there to gather intelligence, observe, not to fix anything or start a new religion. Your brother already died on the cross for everyone's sins," said Father Favian.

"That's a bunch of nonsense," said Soledad. "If he died for everyone's sins, why do these people still have trials and tribulations? Why is the red devil winning? It should have been a straight shot to Paradise; it should have been game over when he died."

Soledad knew she was losing the argument; not because she was wrong, but because the book had already been written and her brother was the One. "Just let me go back for a day. Let me say goodbye to my Mama."

Father Favian diverted his eyes for a second and nodded at Sister Ellen, who crept silently over to Omniscient Observer 1 and screwed off her head. Inside was a Merkaba—a three-dimensional divine light vehicle—two counter-rotating star tetrahedrons pulsing with blue energy fields. Sister Ellen removed the sacred gem and placed it in a box. She screwed the head back on and walked off with the cyborg under her arm.

In the future, a religion was founded on all the things Soledad had said to Freido and Gonzo that were discovered in a cookie jar in the wreckage of an earthquake in Los Angeles. The story was she had died for everyone's sins with no strings attached.

The weight of the world was lifted.

RADIO PANSPERMIA

Televisual glee erupted from the audience crowding Pennsylvania Avenue as the four Dracutians glided down the portico of their spaceship on the White House lawn. The bubble surrounding the pink pod, and its veranda and seven terraces, was only visible in the glint of sunshine bouncing to the heavens. The tall humanoids waved at the crowd and sat down to a feast on the front deck of their dome home.

The putty-faced TV announcer lost his place in the stretch of the unimaginable moment. "We are on the fabulously manicured lawn," said the voice of the teleprompter in his ear.

"We are on the fabulously manicured lawn of the White House on this Good Friday morning, where President Jorge Valentine is expected to make an announcement soon," said Charles. "The Dracutian ambassadors have made the enormous journey from their home star, and they will deliver their message to mankind in just under two hours. First, they will sit down to a magnificent state brunch."

The camera panned out. "This is Charles Azaril, reporting from the White House. Back to you, Elysia." Charles locked his grin on the camera, waiting anxiously for the cut.

"Thanks, Charles. Looks like the crowd is giving those gentlemen a warm welcome," said Elysia. "They must be a bit tired after the long trip. Billions and billions of miles, as the late Carl Sagan would have said."

The station broke for a commercial message touting its special report—BILLIONS AND BILLIONS OF MILES—in super letters across the screen. The marching band from Raleigh, North Carolina, shrank the unthinkable enormity of the voyage into earthling terms with their cymbalic cover of "It's been a hard day's night."

Neena-June Lamb looked away from the kitchen TV and nervously grabbed a sip of coffee. Danté Pilgrim stared in her direction as the microwave beeped his breakfast.

"Life as we know it is over, Danté. I wish life were boring again."

"No, you don't, Neena-June. You're the goddess of discord. You love panic."

"Are you telling me I asked for world chaos?"

The phone rang as Dante danced around the kitchen in his underwear.

"National Press Club, 2 o'clock. Put your pants on," said Neena-June.

At two in the afternoon, Danté and Neena-June

pulled up a barstool at Marvin's on Fourteenth Street for a quick gin and tonic. "Hey, Danté!" said the swarthy bartender, Milton, one of Danté's old work buddies. Neena-June couldn't stand any of Danté's pals from his former life, and Milton couldn't understand Danté's attraction to the abrasive and cynical Miss Lamb.

Neena-June flipped open her laptop and curled the earphone around her ear. President Valentine was just walking up to the podium surrounded by secret service agents. The Fab Four—as the media were now hyping them—waved at the cheering crowd from inside the luminous sphere. The whole scene had a dreamlike feel. Neena-June tried to figure out what exactly was the difference between this and a dream.

She leaned into Danté's ear and asked, "can you get drunk in a dream?"

"I would say not," said Danté, who always answered her as though she was serious, because she usually was. "Somebody else in the dream could be acting drunk, but you couldn't get drunk."

"Why not?"

"Because the dreamer is always drunk. You can't get any drunker."

She put her hand in his back pocket and smiled the first smile of the day. All attention was now fixed on the telescreens in the bar. President Valentine's speech had already begun.

"Our galactic cousins have come in peace as ambassadors of good will. They mean no harm to our people, our customs, our institutions, our religions.

They only wish for us to live in peace, globally and cosmically."

Neena-June listened for shades of nuance in Jorge Valentine's speech. His voice was an octave higher. He stumbled on his words. He was sweating, and he hadn't shaved. Was it really him?

"We should continue our lives in the normal way: Go to work, go to school, go to church, enjoy our sports activities. There has been no real change," said the President. "After all, isn't this what we had supposed all along? Is not God's creation the infinite universe of stars and galaxies—all of them peopled by the same, one God in his infinite purview? And aren't all these people equal in the eyes of our good Creator?"

Jorge Valentine blathered on and on in the clammy oppressive heat. Every person in every sticky collar was itching to hear the cosmic message from the Dracutian emissaries, but it was not to arrive until he had drilled a big, black memory hole where the old insular worldview had been.

Finally, after a dozen or so million-dollar commercials, the camera zoomed in on the Fab Four, who sat in a row on the sofa of their patio. They wore brightly colored Nehru jackets for the unparalleled occasion. The alien leader stepped up to the podium and held up the V sign, the intergalactic symbol of peace, and began speaking in rhythmic English.

"People of Doloré. Friendly greetings from the Limbus borderland to your ground Tartufoli. Downward of seven celestium spheres we fell to visit the

Third Circle Inferno. We thank from our great bosoms your delicious chefs and cheftesses, who are well and truly baked. No people has been so much delight on our lips, twice on the hips. We fatten ourselves to you!"

Hearty laughter emitted from the strangely adolescent face of the leader of the Dracutians. The other three nodded in agreement. Neena-June stared at the TV in horror and looked around the room. All eyes were perched on the screen without a flutter. There was a kind of hush all over the world, as the lanky alien picked up again in the cracking voice of male puberty.

"In peace we bring greetings from Limbus to your teachers of all colors and shapes, to give hugs to your scientists, and in the shining light of Helios to hold your hand. Of vegetable we like many, if your mother likes to ask. For billions and billions of hard days nights we loved your television, your radio, your rock and roll, your Beatles. Now we thank you to sing and dance and play the lyre on the lawn of Khthonia."

The crowd on Pennsylvania Avenue was quiet, except for babies crying and old people asking, "the lawn of where?" The other three lads grinned and gave high fives all around. The leader now introduced himself as George, and his mates as John, Paul and Ringo.

"We like please to have some more TVs, games, and telephones. We like to have three of your guitars, amplifier and drum set. We like to have musical poetry from your Beatles. We like to entertain when the guitars learn to play after some time in the House of the Lie."

"Danté, am I drunk?"

"No, Neena-June, you're not."

She ordered two shots of Johnny Walker, for herself. No wonder the president had looked so strange. The first official ET Open Disclosure had been arranged on his watch, and it was turning into Beatle-gate.

"Oh yes," George came back to the microphone. "We have turned off your guns and weapons, and keep them off, or we will call our big fathers from the Limbus Netherland who will punch out your fathers!"

Just then someone in the crowd hurled a rock at the outlandish couch hobo, which bounced off the electronic bubble. The shield seemed to wobble in the heat and then resumed its rounded shape. George came back with another threat.

"And if you throw rocks or be unruled, you will become our slaves! Do not try to dismantle the big shield, or our big fathers will deliver the Tesla death ray! Thank you. And please deliver some more of those marvelous turkey legs with the Beatle music."

In an instant all the fanfare turned ugly. There was screaming and panic in the streets. All eyes looked to the sky for the impending Tesla death ray. Neena-June's cell phone was ringing like mad. She belted down the two shots and bolted for the door. Danté chased after her, squeezing through the mob that was trying to flee the bar.

One at a time, the crowd at Marvin's popped

out the door into a world of wrong. The natives were running every which way, but there was nowhere to go. The city was crippled. Danté and Neena-June pushed their way through the crowd at the Press Club and flashed their FBI badges. They ran down the hall to the left and knocked on the third door on the right. The door opened and they were rushed inside a chilly room full of intelligence operatives of all stripes.

"Where in hell have you two been?" asked Agent Cerberus.

"Watching from the bar at Marvin's. What do you know so far about these Dracutians?" asked Danté.

"They have shut down all weapons systems globally. All we can do is throw rocks."

Neena-June grinned. "We've been reduced to sticks and stones, just like Einstein said?"

"Apparently so," said the portly Cerberus.

"So, what's the next move?" asked Danté.

"Well, we're keeping them well-fed and entertained until their parents get here," Cerberus tried to keep it serious. They were on their way here as part of the UN's UFO Disclosure Program. We aren't sure what's happening with that plan now.

"Aren't their fathers heading here to punch ... ?" Danté trailed off, feeling suddenly foolish.

"The Dracutians are in the 5b Sector Treaty group," explained Cerberus, in his usual deadpan delivery. "They cannot land on the White House lawn and start demanding turkey legs and Beatle music."

"Oh, but they have," said Neena-June.

"We think these kids put it in warp drive, so to speak, and arrived here before their parents," explained the chief, Guelph Blackmon, stepping into the circle of conversation. "We were expecting the mother ship. This is the—ah, I guess you'd call it—the birth pod."

"Or the teenage space van," Danté chided. Nobody was in the mood to laugh.

"We think it escaped from the group," said Cerberus, waddling over to a chair to take the load off. "They don't usually travel in lone ships like this. Especially the student scout ships. These kids are in a lick of trouble."

"Oh, good lord," said Neena-June. "So, they aren't really dangerous?"

"We're not sure about that, but at this point it wouldn't be easy to convince the public, even if it were true," replied Guelph.

"Exactly," Cerberus interrupted. "There's sheer hysteria out there. And when they see the fleet of ships coming to collect the kids, there's gonna be a real panic."

"What's the plan? Can't you call and have their parents ground them?" Neena-June mocked.

"That's the wild card," answered Guelph. "We don't know their parenting style. We're waiting to hear from the NSC. There's pizza in the conference room. Go and relax while you can. We need you here the rest of the night."

Neena-June sat by the stack of pizzas and shivered. The air conditioning was turned up way too high. Cerberus was already on his third slice. Air whistled through his nostrils and grease dribbled down his chin.

Just then Guelph entered the conference room and instructed everyone to sit and watch the replay of George's speech. "We need all hands on deck. Freestyle, what's going on here?"

"That bubble. Can we hit it with anything?" asked Danté.

"Everything's shut down. We're waiting to hear whether HAARP in Alaska is still operational," said Guelph.

"HAARP!" Danté flipped. "Yeah, let's make a hole in the sky and let the sun pan fry the whole city!"

"Well, if the dads come down and decide we haven't been nice to the kids, we might have to use it to intercept their missiles," Cerberus retorted, munching on his fourth slice.

"All right, you two. Let's back up to George's first words," Neena-June offered calmly. "Doloré is Italian for Earth. Limbus is Italian for Limbo. Where are these kids getting this Medieval metaphysical language?"

"Good point," said Cerberus. "They've been on a ship absorbing television and radio since they were born. They must have all the languages and dialects of Earth down by now."

"What is that word he used right there? Tartufoli?" asked Danté.

"That's Italian for potato," replied Cerberus, with a piece of pepperoni wagging from his lip.

"People, we're through the looking glass here," declared Guelph. "This is a home invasion. Some teenagers from Hell have the White House by the short hairs."

I'm not so sure that's where they're from, thought Neena-June. She wanted to correct the metaphysical direction but thought better of it for now.

"What's the first move?" asked Danté.

"There it is," said Guelph, rewinding the video to where George requested three guitars, three amplifiers and a drum set.

"Is there a guitar shop opened?" said Guelph. "Cerberus, make some calls. Neena-June and Danté, you're making the delivery. Let's get going."

"What about the sheet music and turkey legs?" asked Neena-June.

"Yup, let's go *all* out," ordered Guelph.

It was dusk by the time the van pulled up in the alley stocked with the Dracutian grocery order. The CIA driver they had assigned to Beatlegate was Leon Nolan, a black man with a huge Afro, wearing truly, short shorts. Neena-June had worked with him before he had the Afro. *Oh shit*, she thought. *This is weird.*

To make things weirder, they were told to pretend Agent Nolan was a slave, because Dracutians have slaves, and they would think it was the normal way to do things. The last thing the U.S. government wanted, Guelph had advised, was to make the kids lean on some kind of button in there. "They won't understand that we do things ourselves here, so don't help him carry anything," he ordered.

Neena-June didn't believe the Fab Four were hostile. *I'll make that judgment when I get in there,* she thought. She climbed up into the passenger seat of the beat-up van and checked out the dashboard saints amidst glittery stars.

"Hey, Nolan, how've you been?" She checked her list up against his. "So, you've got guitars and everything, hey Nolan? Good show."

"Nolan, how many amps you got?" yelled Danté, sitting on a guitar amp in the back of the tripped-out van.

"Well, I did the best I could," said Nolan. "The stores were closing. I got three guitars, one amp."

"The four have to share an amp?" said Danté sarcastically.

There was silence in the van for a few blocks. Nolan had done the best he could and was pissed at the wisecrack. Danté broke the silence. "Well, Nolan, thanks for picking up all this stuff. You did a great job."

"Yes, Nolan, thank you," Neena-June agreed. "Have you been briefed on all this yet?"

"Not really," he responded. "I got a short briefing from Cerberus about a call to their parents. He said the kids have shut down global weapons systems. Remarkable! How did they do that?"

Danté tried to explain. "All we know is the Dracutian command ships were on their way here as part of the UN's UFO Disclosure Program, and we're not sure how this is possible, but apparently they hadn't realized they lost one of their radio pods with the kids inside."

"The Dracutian parents have now seen the TV broadcasts of the event and seem to understand the ramifications," added Neena-June. "We're not sure if they're still coming or canceling the meeting."

"What a trip!" smirked Nolan. "How long ago did they lose the pod? Wait a minute, radio pod?"

"Just my theory, explained Danté. "Did you see the size of the antenna sticking out of that thing?"

"Yeah, can you dig it? The babysitters lost the kids!" said Neena-June.

Nolan laughed. "Cerberus mentioned something about a treaty. Where does that play out?"

"Yup, the 5b Sector Treaty is an agreement by ET groups who agree to leave a system alone unless invited by its ruling authority," explained Neena-June. "It's laid out in the guise of free will, but it doesn't allow anyone to step in to secure the choices available. So, it's top-down free will."

"Which doesn't sound to me like free will," yelled Danté from the back, over the van's loud muffler.

"But how much of this did the Fab Four cause themselves?" asked Nolan. "Don't they have a direct dial button in there to call mom and dad?"

"Don't know what kind of buttons or dials they have in there. That's what we're going in to find out," replied Danté.

"Don't forget. They've got so-called free will," explained Neena-June. "They can choose to hit whatever button they want to hit. Or not. But they changed the structure of the material universe by choosing to do nothing, which actually is a choice. They've flipped the concept of 'directed' panspermia into its inadvertent form, 'radio' panspermia, which is a fall by light pressure from above."

Danté shouted from the back, "Yeah. Is this the fall of the innocent, or were they sent here for some ulterior purpose? That's the wild card."

Nolan grinned, passing around a fat joint. Neena-June passed on it, but handed it to Danté, who freely imbibed. "Oh yeah, so, you know, Guelph Blackmon wants you to play the slave, right?"

Nolan exhaled a big puff of weed and coughed. "What? He mentioned me doing all the lugging, but the black man didn't have the gall to use the S-word with another black man. What's with that?"

"Well, from what I understand," replied Neena-June, "the Dracutians have a hierarchical, caste system with specific job designations. The chief thought a 'like you, like me' scenario would aid the bonding process."

"I'm sorry, Nolan," Neena-June turned toward him, her eyes big with sorrow. "If it's any consolation, we are all slaves to the government. Use the S-word as your Sword."

"The Kingdom of God is Anarchy. The Center is Everywhere," replied Nolan.

As they swung around the secret, back entrance to the White House, they came upon an army of black guard dogs. They handed over their ID's to a military goon and the gate swung open. Just around the corner, as the pink biodome came into view, Neena-June and Danté were pulled running from the van.

"Do you have the guitars?" they were grilled loudly by white-haired Army Intel officer, Colonel Charon, with fiery red eyes from lack of sleep.

"We must treat these children as heads of state from another world!" Charon shouted. "They have waited way too long for these items! They have every right to call their parents, except that they're runaways and *we're* the ones that had to call *their* parents! This is the most messed up situation I've ever seen in my life!" he screamed. "That's probably why I'm screaming!" he screamed.

"Yes, I understand, sir. Let's not delay any further," Neena-June responded, still startled by the up-close sight of the pink radio pod. "We're going in."

She motioned to Nolan in the van. He had pulled up to the edge of the grass and was waiting for instructions. Charon glanced at him and did a double-take at his giant mane. "Oh, of course. Have him drive right on the grass behind us and wait outside for your call."

As Charon led the two ambassadors to the lower terrace of the craft, Nolan made the sign of the cross in the air as he whispered, "God Bless the transport of Intrepid Souls."

"Stand here in the inner circle," Charon instructed. "I've been in, and it's completely painless. The radio scanner simply reads your natal frequency ID and carries you in." He put their hands together and, in the fierce brightness of an ecstatic moment, the two were ferried up to the pod like waves on a beach. Faces first, they squeaked through a seamless, liquid aperture with the sound of a balloon popping.

There was nobody home. The huge, round room seemed much bigger than it looked from outside. There were four separate apartments with four separate everythings. Neena-June looked for mirrors but couldn't tell if there were any. Just then the four lads entered the room at the same time through four different doors. They each flopped onto their own sofa and clicked on their own TV.

Danté chortled uncontrollably. Neena-June cast him a baleful glance. Finally, George noticed them. "Oh, our guests are here!"

"Hello. I'm Neena-June Lamb. This is Danté Pilgrim. We have your guitars and your turkey legs just outside. Would you like me to call the slave to bring those?"

"You have slave? Yes, we want to see your slave with the turkey legs," said Paul.

Danté lost it again. *Oh god*, thought Neena-June, *I'm on my own here*.

She rang Nolan. "Come on in. They want to see your turkey legs," she told him. While she had the phone out, Neena-June asked, "Hey boys, can I get a picture of you to show my mom?"

Sure. They moved closer together. "Your mom knows us?" asked Paul.

"Are we more popular than Jesus Christ?" asked John, as pictures and sound were transmitted to the CIA headquarters in Langley.

"Yes, I would say so," said Danté.

Neena-June asked for another picture, this time for her dad. They put their heads together for another instant transmission. The lads seemed to be all about moms and dads. They seemed homesick and were overeating to the point of gluttony. George grabbed a can of spray, whipped cream out of the box Nolan carried in through the waterwall. "Must we shake well?"

"Yes, you *do* need to shake that well," explained Danté in the most helpful tone he could muster without losing it again.

"Contains dairy?" asked George, as he shook it and sprayed a big, overflowing mouthful.

"Yes, it *does* contain dairy," Danté advised. They both looked at George aghast. *How do all teenagers know how to do that?* Neena-June wondered.

Ringo picked up a jar of mayonnaise and stared at the barcode. "Barcode is radio I.D. in stripes like zebra?"

"Something like that," Neena-June responded, sneaking a glance at Danté.

Paul studied the barcode on the ketchup bottle. "Slave, is this ketchup boy or girl?" he asked Nolan.

"I think it's a girl," Nolan smiled, as he swashed through the waterwall to fetch another box. This was the most effortless delivery he had ever made. He simply modulated through the waterwall carrying one box at a time.

The couch bums were baffled by everything they touched. "Hey, wait! Are you mod squads from television?" asked John from his sofa eating a turkey leg.

Nolan turned and vanished again through the waterwall, chuckling as he modulated through space. As Neena-June and Danté were quizzed by the innocence mission, a beamish joy overwashed them.

Just then the pod rang with a trumpet blast. A female voice blared into each of the apartments summoning the Fab Four by their real names. Homer, Ovid, Lucan and Horace wiped whipped cream off their faces and hid the turkey legs behind their backs.

A magnificent dignitary as deep blue as the god Krishna appeared as a hologram. His jacket was deep orange saffron and on the left breast was the official insignia of the solar disk. Above that, his name read: Virgil. He spoke in a sublime cadence, a fantastic rising and falling language.

—Zap!

Neena-June's golden hair stood jazzed in the ethericity. Struck dumb in the aphonia of an ethereal thunderclap, her fingers reached for Danté's with great effort, as the bowl of heaven quickened with a hundred sacred names of god. And that was just the hello.

To the earthling nebbishes caught in the superhet, it took an eternity for the delivery of the heliogram,

—a drama in miniature,

—a narration in a shadow play.

In this, the blue representative was assisted by a team of Telestai, Poets of Projection Science whose stunning logograms had never been unscrambled by enemy ciphernauds.

The poets removed their robes, which plunked to the floor and disappeared. In blue body tights, they expertly mimed the cosmic fiasco of the runaway egg to an invisible audience of government officials. They emoted with hand signals and ballistic pokes and slaps, while making vocal sounds and pharting with hands cupped in armpits.

Once the debacle of the early birthing and the lack of fetal training had been elucidated, various faults widened the crack in the egg: the disaster at the House of the Lie, the impish hellions who threw rocks at the pod, the radio talk shows blaring around heaven's dome poking fun of the "cowardly neutrals" who had lost their children—as the joke went—in a downward motion, *panspermia perpetuum celestium motuum*.

Every Telestai finger touched a new sore spot; every slap produced a bruise of embarrassment. They must now decide. The debates of imperial counsel were moderated by a new wave of moral absolutism. The children had behaved badly, but there was a right and a wrong thing to do now.

With sudden and grotesque efficiency, the voting buttons conveyed the swift command.

—Go!
—Take them!
—Now!

Only then were the insensate bugs in the mute amber-theatre released from the glue that held them.

George walked over and tried to explain:

"Our moms and dads remind us that we are Kings of the Seven-Terraces of the Purgatory-Limbus Borderland, not prisoners of scandalous condiments of the gluttonous Third Ring of Hades. Our senators tell us to rise above with no more fooling around, so we must heed immediately. Please sit and fasten your seatbelts, Mr. Danté Aligheri and Ms. Jesus Christos. I'm sorry to tell you we must leave Mr. Giordano Bruno here, as his product code has not been upgraded in the free will system."

Back at the van, Nolan felt a jolt of energy and then sudden inertia. He shook the electricity out of his hands, picked up the Fender Telecaster and moved slowly toward the dock. He stood there a while, but the freq-net seemed to be shut down.

What he didn't know was his radio freq tag was phant-scat—a scattered phantom signal rejected by the Babylon system. It was a violation of the 5b Sector Treaty to apprehend a slave.

As he stared up at the incredible radio pod, it suddenly retracted its long antenna and began to pulse like a jellyfish. Before it shot vertically into the heavens, it hovered a few seconds on the White House lawn to pull in the patio furniture and neaten up the back forty.

With his arms held out as a shadow in the twilight of sunrise, the Great Nolan, Giordano Bruno, blessed them on their journey: "Cabala of the Steed like unto Pegasus!"

On Easter Sunday, the *Washington Post* described the remains of a hot pink weather balloon that had set off the national security apparatus. It had been a 'hoax', of course—a computer-generated simulation by Asian students from M.I.T.

The four pranksters were arrested without delay. Just below their pictures on the front page, the *Post* reported that the President was recovering, his doctor said, from a slight touch of swamp gas.

Another curious story on the back page reported an anomalous sighting of Jimi Hendrix wandering the streets with a Telecaster. But as everyone knows, Jimi played a Stratocaster.

BOOKS BY THIS AUTHOR

Huntergatheress Journal

Joan d'Arc and Friends: A collection of fiction, non-fiction and poetry from the Middle Stoned Age (Vol 1, 2008)

Phenomenal World

Remote viewing, astral travel, apparitions, extraterrestrials, lucid dreams and other forms of intelligent contact in the Magical Kingdom of Mind-at-Large

Space Travelers And The Genesis Of The Human Form

Evidence of Intelligent Contact in the Solar System

The Conspiracy Reader

The Conspiracy Reader: From the Deaths of JFK and John Lennon to Government-Sponsored Alien Cover-

ups

The Complete Conspiracy Reader

The Complete Conspiracy Reader: From the Deaths of JFK and John Lennon to Government-Sponsored Alien Coverups

The New Conspiracy Reader

The New Conspiracy Reader: From Planet X to the War on Terrorism-What You Really Don't Know Paperback

Paranoia: The Conspiracy Reader, Volume 1

PARANOIA compendium, 24 authors and interviewees discuss the monumental conspiracies of our time
· Did the Mob assassinate JFK? · Who is reabducting UFO abductees? · What role do magick and ritual play in The Invisible Government? · Have we received any messages from space?

Conspiracy Geek

Collected writings and interviews. Sisyphus Press, 2012. Out of print.

Made in the USA
Middletown, DE
12 October 2020

21727550R00110